Billionaires for the Rose Sisters

A brand-new duet from Rachael Stewart

Life hasn't been so kind to sisters Jessie and Hannah Rose recently. The loss of their mother and betrayals of the men they once loved have left them both reeling; romance is the last thing on either of their minds. Until billionaire best friends Joel Austin and Brendan Hart upend all their plans...

Read Jessie and Joel's story in
Billionaire's Island Temptation

And don't miss Hannah and Brendan's story
Consequence of Their Forbidden Night

Both available now!

Dear Reader,

I love an unrequited love story that evolves into a HEA. In this case, Hannah is so fiercely guarded over her heart and her control that she won't let love in. She marries for all the wrong reasons the first time around, and Brendan's been a patient man, waiting for her to come to her senses. But now the gloves are off—she's a free woman and he's going after his heart's desire...

As for Hannah, she's a workaholic big sister who feels the weight of that responsibility to her soul. She might not be your cup of tea to begin with—in fact, I guarantee she won't be—but bear with her. She has her reasons for behaving the way she does. She's an alpha heroine with a big heart—if only she'd give it the freedom to love. She's on a steep learning curve emotionally, but with Brendan showing her the way, she's in safe and very skilled hands... ;-)

Be warned—these two are smoking hot when they come together, but it's their absolute love for one another that binds them in the end. I hope you love them as much as I do.

Rachael xx

Consequence of Their Forbidden Night

Rachael Stewart

Recycling programs
for this product may
not exist in your area.

ISBN-13: 978-1-335-73713-7

Consequence of Their Forbidden Night

Copyright © 2023 by Rachael Stewart

All rights reserved. No part of this book may be used or reproduced in
any manner whatsoever without written permission except in the case of
brief quotations embodied in critical articles and reviews.

This is a work of fiction. Names, characters, places and incidents
are either the product of the author's imagination or are used fictitiously.
Any resemblance to actual persons, living or dead, businesses,
companies, events or locales is entirely coincidental.

For questions and comments about the quality of this book,
please contact us at CustomerService@Harlequin.com.

Harlequin Enterprises ULC
22 Adelaide St. West, 41st Floor
Toronto, Ontario M5H 4E3, Canada
www.Harlequin.com

Printed in U.S.A.

Rachael Stewart adores conjuring up stories, from heartwarmingly romantic to wildly erotic. She's been writing since she could put pen to paper—as the stacks of scrawled-on pages in her loft will attest to. A Welsh lass at heart, she now lives in Yorkshire, with her very own hero and three awesome kids—and if she's not tapping out a story, she's wrapped up in one or enjoying the great outdoors. Reach her on Facebook, Twitter (@rach_b52) or at rachaelstewartauthor.com.

Books by Rachael Stewart

Harlequin Romance

Billionaires for the Rose Sisters

Billionaire's Island Temptation

Claiming the Ferrington Empire

Secrets Behind the Billionaire's Return
The Billionaire Behind the Headlines

Tempted by the Tycoon's Proposal
Surprise Reunion with His Cinderella
Beauty and the Reclusive Millionaire
My Year with the Billionaire

Harlequin DARE

Reawakened

Visit the Author Profile page at Harlequin.com.

For all the Big Sisters out there... xxx

Praise for
Rachael Stewart

CHAPTER ONE

HANNAH ROSE STARED at the papers in her hand, willing them to disappear. The words bounced around, letters scattering but always reuniting in the same order: DIVORCE.

Leon had filed for divorce. Eight years and it was over.

Perfect Marriage. Perfect Home. Perfect Life. Done.

Note that she didn't say Perfect Husband.

Because he'd never been that…

She'd been happy to pretend though. The other 'P' she was always so great at…

Perfection and Pretence.

But there could be no pretence now.

Divorce.

Everyone would know her failure.

At least Mum wasn't around to witness it, her accident a few years back and subsequent death four months ago one of the many reasons Hannah had kept her marital breakdown to herself. And her little sister didn't need to learn of it. Her sister didn't need this to add to the steaming pot of despair she was already swimming in.

That's it, blame your sister, your need to protect her, when the truth is you haven't wanted to acknowledge it. You haven't wanted to face it.

She swallowed the rising sob as she accepted it, accepted it and recalled the conversation she'd had with her best friend, Brendan, over a year ago now. A conversation in which he'd told her of Leon's affairs and she'd all but closed the door on him and buried her head in the sand.

But there could be no more burying, no more denying...

Her stomach rolled and she clutched the papers to it, struggling to breathe, to see beyond the debris of her life to a future she hadn't planned.

She needed Brendan. She needed to talk to him. He was the only one that could understand, the only one that knew it all.

And don't you think you're a year too late?

Ignoring the inner gibe, she tugged her suitcase from her closet and started throwing in clothes. She would go to New York, she would speak to Brendan, he knew her and he knew Leon, he would help her make sense of it.

And you really think seeing Brendan when you're wired up like a Christmas tree is a good idea?

She ignored that too.

Yes, they had chemistry.

Yes, he set her alight with a simple look.

But she was also married, for now at any rate,

and quite capable of keeping that Pandora's box firmly closed.

Absolutely, unequivocally in control of it all…

Except you're not.

Brendan Hart stared at the blonde woman striding across his living room as though she were an apparition because she might as well be. Her ivory silk blouse, white skirt, nude heels all adding to the ghost-like impression…

He hadn't seen her in months, and even then, it had been a glimpse in the office, a strained exchange at her mother's funeral, nothing more. Because more would suggest their friendship was unbroken. More would suggest that the conversation they'd had over a year ago had never happened. She had taken his words of concern and dismissed them as if they meant nothing. As if her husband's affairs meant nothing.

'Brendan?' His name on her lips was a gasp, an uncertain whisper, her blue-grey eyes slaying him with their pain, their uncertainty. What had happened to make her look like so? And why did he have to care so damn much?

He moved before he could give it all away—the hurt, the pain…the unrequited love. His forceful stride matching the staccato of his heart as he headed for his drinks cabinet.

He didn't ask, just poured—two glasses, two fingers—and turned, holding one whisky out to her.

She wet her lips, pale pink and glossy—the same colour as the nails on her fingers as she reached out to take the glass, careful not to brush his own. 'Thank you.'

'Why are you here, Hannah?'

No preamble, no 'How are you?' Her eyes widened a fraction, but he was done being soft, done being gentle.

She lifted her chin, those eyes he'd dreamed of far too often wavering as she held his eye and followed his lead. 'Did you know Leon's filed for divorce?'

Leon. The last person on earth he wanted to talk about. Especially with her.

He shook his head, walked away. 'Why would I know that?'

He didn't stop until he was before the floor-to-ceiling glass, his eyes trained on the glittering Manhattan skyline and not the woman who dropped to the sofa behind him. His jaw throbbed, its clenched state doing him no favours. But what was the other option? Tell her the truth, let it all come out, and to hell with the consequences.

'How could he do it, Brendan, after all this time?'

He stiffened, disbelief holding his tongue. Of all the questions to ask…

The man had had a litany of affairs, their marriage had been a farce for long enough already.

The real question was why had Leon done it and not her?

'Brendan?'

He ground his teeth, sensed her red-rimmed eyes spear him, could make out her blurred reflection in the glass, an enticing ivory blot in the midnight blue.

He never should have let her in. Should have taken his concierge's concerned tone as warning enough. But it was too late for that wisdom now. She was in, and she was under his skin.

A renowned criminal defence attorney, orphaned heir to what was now—thanks to him—a billion-dollar hotel empire, he didn't crack under pressure, he didn't lose his cool…but Hannah…

She had the power to undo him. And after more than a decade of caging his feelings, he was about to let loose, and all because *she* was unhinged. For the first time in all the years he'd known her, *she* was crumbling. All because a man who didn't deserve her was leaving her.

He swallowed the incredulous laugh that wanted to erupt and lifted his whisky to his lips, took a lingering sip.

'*Brendan?* Talk to me!'

His knuckles flashed white around the crystal in his hand, his head shifting just enough to show he wasn't deaf…

'And I repeat, why did you come here, Hannah?'

'Why?' Her voice was as strained as he felt. 'Because you're the only one who knows what's going on, the only one I can talk to who will understand.'

He couldn't contain the laugh now, harsh, cutting. 'And that's where you're wrong. I don't understand. I didn't understand a year ago and I understand even less now.'

The subtle music he'd been playing before she arrived filled the silence and he resisted the urge to fill it. To take it back. To go to her. To soothe her. To do what he always did…

'I *need* you, Brendan.' Her whispered words carried on the melody, her soft confession licking fire through his veins. Words he'd craved once upon a time. Words his body still craved and reacted to even as his head inserted her real meaning. Her very platonic meaning.

With a rigid spine, he went back to the view.

'You don't need me, Hannah.' He took a sip of whisky, cherishing the burn. 'Like everything in your life, you'll deal with it and move on.'

He sensed her tense as he hit his mark. 'How can you say that?'

The need to take it back clambered up within him. The need to apologise, to get them back to safer ground…but what good would it do? He'd spent too many years holding his tongue, waiting on the periphery for her to wake up only to realise she'd been awake all along…awake and just didn't care.

Until now.

'Because it's the truth.'

'I thought you of all people would understand. You know Leon and you know me, you're the only one who can help me make sense of it.'

He scoffed, his head shaking. 'You couldn't be more wrong.'

'But you were the one who came to me.'

'I came to you over a year ago!' he interjected, grimacing at the force with which he'd exploded and working to ease his tone, his posture. 'If you'd reacted like this then, I'd understand, but now…'

'It was different then.'

'How was it different?'

'He wasn't demanding a divorce.'

His smile was a snarl on his lips. 'Something you should have been doing. Not him.'

'I know, Brendan, I know.'

'Do you? Because I came to you and told you he was having an affair and you blinked it away like I'd told you a client had taken their business elsewhere…' Another laugh as he realised the truth. 'No, in fact, you would have fought to get them back. With Leon…you just let it slide.'

'I didn't let it slide, I—it's not like I didn't care…'

'You just didn't care enough?'

'How could I? Mum was dying. Jess was a mess. The Clarence case had imploded. I didn't have the capacity to deal with it.'

'The *capacity*? We're talking about your marriage, Hannah. Love. Not some case that needs heavy manpower behind it. Can you not see what's wrong with this picture?'

'Wrong with me, you mean?'

'You said it, not me.'

She took a shaky breath, her pain so evident and so rare to witness, but he refused to take it back.

'You've barely lived on the same continent for the past two years, Hannah. It's hardly the sign of a couple fighting to save their marriage, so why is his filing for divorce such a shock now?'

'I don't know, Brendan, I just…' She hung her head in her hands. 'The truth is I could cope with the infidelity. I didn't like it but so long as he kept it quiet, and—'

'You could *cope*? Have you heard yourself?'

'I know how it sounds.'

'I don't think you do.'

'Put yourself in my shoes, Brendan. I've lived my life projecting perfection and protecting my family as I did so. I *needed* to have it under control and we were doing fine, we were…'

'Fine?' His laugh rebounded off the glass, cold with disdain. 'Is that what you call living a lie?'

'There was no lie.'

'No? So, playing happy families was—'

'No, not happy families, we were never going to have children.'

Another scoff. 'Thank God for that.'

'Brendan!' she blurted, the delicate shift of fabric and air telling him she was on the move. Coming closer. 'You have to understand…'

'You keep saying that, but it doesn't make it true.'

He could feel the approaching warmth of her body, his own tensing, preparing itself for the inevitable shift in heart rate, heat, awareness…all for her.

'Please, Brendan, don't do this. Don't judge me. The last few years have been a blur. With Jessie's breakdown, Mum's accident then—then losing her, and now Leon's upped and left, I couldn't bear it if I lost you too.'

He took another sip of whisky to prevent the denial that wanted to erupt, the hands that wanted to reach for her and reassure her because she could never lose him… No matter how much distance he'd inserted over the years, she'd always managed to cross it.

'You're hardly losing me.'

'You sure about that?' It was all husky and full of feeling. 'You've been so aloof since Mum's funeral. Before then even…'

Because he'd had to be…seeing her become ever more closed off, emotionally and physically, knowing what was happening behind closed doors, behind the perfect front. It wasn't because he didn't care.

'I've been busy,' he said simply. 'You know that.'

'You've always been busy…' she touched a palm

to his upper arm, the contact burning through the thin fabric of his shirt '…not distant.'

He eyed her hand, wishing its electrifying effect away. 'If you think I've been distant, why choose to come to me now?'

'Because I can't bear it any more. My life is falling apart and you're the only one I can turn to.'

His heart pulsed, cherishing her words even though they were born of panic, an alien uncertainty that thrummed off her in waves. He'd never seen her this broken. Even at her mother's funeral she'd been stoic, solid for her sister, composed for the room, just as she'd been that first day he'd met her. Fifteen years ago, at a lecture with Leon. She'd been speaking as an Oxford graduate to a room full of hopefuls. The women all wanting to be her, the men all wanting to bed her, and he'd been no different.

Leon had been gushing about her before their arrival. Smitten and ridiculous with it. But the moment Brendan had seen her, he'd fared no better.

And then, she'd spoken. So eloquent and knowledgeable, the right level of passion, the right level of enthusiasm for justice in a world that simply wasn't fair, a world that had failed his own parents. He'd been enraptured, spellbound with the entire room as they'd witnessed a world-class lawyer in the making.

A woman so far removed from the one breaking down in his room now and taking his heart with her.

'What am I going to do?'

He took a steadying breath. 'You're going to give him the divorce he wants and put it behind you.'

Her fingers twitched upon his arm and he stepped away, creating the distance his head and heart needed, but his body loathed. 'Why is it so hard, Hannah? You knew your marriage was over a long time ago.'

'I'll have to tell Jess and I can't bear to have her worrying about me.'

'But it's okay for you to worry about her twenty-four-seven?'

'I don't—okay, okay, I do. But she's my little sister and she's not good, Brendan. She's already locked herself away at home, surrounded by Mum's stuff, she's given up her life in London and I have no idea how to snap her out of it.'

Worry tremored through her and he got it. For all the time he'd known her, Hannah had always put her mother and sister first. And now she only had her sister left, everything was for her. And so, he believed her when she said Jess was her biggest concern, but…

'She's a grown woman, Hannah, she'll find her way.'

'You can't know that, not with her history, and I don't know what I can do to help her. If she'd just take a holiday, do something to get away for a bit, a break from the house and all of Mum's things, at least I'd feel like she was moving forward, but she refuses.'

'Then make her an offer she can't refuse.'

'Like?'

He couldn't stop himself from coming to her aid, a solution quick to form... 'She can use my place in Mustique. Staff, travel costs, all of it covered. It makes no odds to me, but it could make all the difference for her.'

'You'd seriously do that for me?'

'For you, for her...' He shrugged as though it were nothing but his heart knew it was indicative of so much more. 'I'm not using it and to many it would be the holiday of a lifetime.'

'It would, but—'

'But what, Hannah? If it'll help her and in turn help you...'

He shouldn't have turned. He shouldn't have taken in her choked-up gaze. 'Thank you.'

He nodded, unable to trust his voice. Hating that she made him so weak. So vulnerable. And feeling it all the same.

'How can I repay you?'

'You don't,' he ground out. 'Not financially. But you need to come clean with her. If she's anything like you, your happiness will be all she cares about and once she gets over her shock, she'll want you to find it, again. Whatever happiness looks like for you.' Because it wasn't the average person's view of happiness, of that he couldn't be more sure. 'And let's be honest, the last thing Jessie would want is for you to remain married to that man after all he has done.'

'That man?' Her eyes were wide once more. 'Since when have you spoken about Leon like that? He's your friend.'

'*Was*, Hannah, he *was* my friend. Do you honestly think I could stand by and watch how he treated you and remain so? We've hardly spoken in years…which you'd have noticed if you'd taken off those rose-tinted spectacles you insist on wearing.'

She frowned. 'That's hardly fair.'

'Isn't it?'

'Every time I caught some tension between the pair of you, I questioned you or him, and you both told me all was fine.'

'We told you what you wanted to hear, Hannah, for that I am as guilty as he and I'm sorry, but we haven't been friends in a long time. As for your marriage, that's been over almost as long, surely you can see that?'

The man had abused their marriage, taken her for a mug right under her nose. He thought back to their conversation a year ago, recalled her cool, calm demeanour as he'd admitted what he knew, and the realisation smacked him in the face.

'You already knew, didn't you?' He rounded on

her. How had he not realised? How had he been so blind to it? Some infamous defence attorney he was when he couldn't spot the lie right in front of his face. 'Back then, when I came to you, you already knew he was playing away?'

She struggled to swallow, the delicate skin of her throat revealing so much.

'Answer me, Hannah.'

She didn't have a tell in the courtroom, but she wouldn't fool the most novice of poker tables now.

'Hannah!'

'Yes! Yes, I knew.'

His stomach rolled, but his eyes were unblinking as they speared her. 'And you didn't think to tell me when I came to you? Do you know how hard it was for me to do that? Knowing all that you had going on? How sick your mother was? How responsible you felt for both her and your sister, burning the candles at both ends to meet the demands of your job and your family? To add to that burden...'

'I'm sorry, Brendan, I should have told you. But I—I was blindsided. It was one thing me knowing, another having you...*you* of all people come to me.'

A tremble worked its way through her body and his jaw pulsed, the urge to pull her to his chest, to comfort her, burning through his fingers and instead he threw that passion into his words.

'You gave me nothing, Hannah! No emotion, no

reassurance, no nothing!' He turned away, raked a hand through his hair as his mind travelled back in time. 'You know I called him out on it, don't you?'

Silence, and he spun to face her, her stricken face doing nothing to ease his rage, his pain, as with a trembling hand she raised her drink to her lips, gulped at it.

'I told him he needed to come clean, that he couldn't do this to you. And he told me, *he* told me, you knew. He said who was the one doing the dirty really? Him playing away from home or the wife who insisted on projecting a lie? And I *defended* you. I refused to believe him while trying to convince him to do right by you.'

His body shook with it all. It was their job to hide their feelings, to prevent the sweat pricking at their necks breaking their brow, but this was personal, and his body was exposing the whole damn lot.

'I'm sorry, Brendan.' She tried to reach for him but he backed away. 'I should've told you the truth and explained.'

He wasn't listening. 'How long had you known?'

She wet her lips. 'Long enough.'

Ice rushed his veins—confusion, disbelief, anger playing havoc with his bloodstream. 'A month, two, a year even?'

Her eyes flitted to his, guilt a storm within the grey as she refused to answer.

'Before your mother's accident?' The only excuse he could think to give her at the time, her mother's ill health, and yet her face all but told him otherwise. He cursed. 'You're unbelievable!'

'I had an inkling. That was all.' She was trying to backtrack. He could read it in her gaze as readily as he could read a jury. 'We—we were spending so much time on different continents and when we were together, there was no…passion.' She fumbled over the word, her cheeks colouring, the flush to her chest where the ivory silk parted tugging at his gaze, going against his anger, his better judgement. 'Discovering he was finding it elsewhere could hardly be a surprise.'

'And you think that makes it okay? That it justifies his behaviour? I didn't see *you* finding that passion elsewhere.'

'I didn't say that it was okay. And it was more of a suspicion than a certainty. I figured we were tired, work was busy, we rarely had a moment to catch our breath, but then I found the credit card statements, the dinners for two… Hotel rooms I could ignore, we always booked suites, it didn't mean we had company, but the jewellery stores and the flowers, they were the giveaways. I think he wanted me to find out, leaving a trail under my nose so I'd be forced to have it out with him, or maybe he wanted to provoke a rise out of me. Either way, I knew it was coming to a head.'

'And instead, you gave him nothing? Just like you did me.'

Her eyes flashed. 'No, not like you, never like you.'

'And what's that supposed to mean?'

'You're my best friend, Brendan.'

'And he was—*is* your husband.'

'And he's finally found the love of his life in someone else and left me.'

'You left each other a long time ago.'

'I was willing to carry on.'

'Are you serious, Hannah?'

'I know how it sounds. I know.'

'Do you? Because from where I'm standing you sound like you care more about appearances than you do anything else.'

'Because appearances *are everything*. They're what kept my mother and sister on the straight and narrow, what convinced the world that I'm a lawyer to be trusted, what got me where I am now and convinced *me* that I had my life in hand.'

'And now Leon wants a divorce, you think you've lost that?'

'I've lost *everything*, Brendan.' The tremor to her voice tore through him. He could cope with stoic Hannah. He could cope with the composed Hannah that had barely batted an eyelid over her husband's extramarital affairs. He might have walked away and not understood it, but he could deal with it.

This version though…

'Losing a man that loves another isn't losing everything, Hannah.' He took another swig of whisky as he forced the truth out. 'You need to gain some perspective.'

She gave a pitched laugh. 'I have plenty of perspective, Brendan, and if you think these tears are over him, you're wrong. It's everything. Mum's gone. Jessie is alone after Adam upped and left her. My life is falling apart at the seams and I'm supposed to be the solid one, the one with everything in hand, the responsible one. I'm supposed to be looking out for my sister, not the other way around. Now we're both—we're both—'

'You're both going to be fine, Hannah, because guess what, staying in a loveless relationship isn't healthy for anyone.'

'And what would you know of it? I've known you over a decade and you've never had one that lasted longer than five minutes.'

His shoulders twitched, her words a direct hit.

'I'm sorry, I shouldn't have said that. It's none of my business.'

'And yet, you said it anyway.'

Would she have said it if she knew the truth? That the reason no woman had lasted more than 'five minutes' was because no woman could obliterate her from his mind?

'I'm sorry, Brendan, truly I am. I'm just— I'm so lost.' She buried her head in her hand, the whisky sloshing as she physically crumbled before him. 'I can't believe this is happening. After all this time, he wants to throw our life away on some woman he's only just met.'

'Some woman he loves,' he ground out, reminding her of that important fact.

'Apparently so...' she whispered as though giving it more volume would only hammer the truth home. Or was it more that she didn't believe it herself?

'You don't believe him?'

'I don't know what to think.'

'Try telling yourself that you deserve more, Hannah. You deserve a man who will take the time to cherish you, to worship you...' His hand lifted to palm her cheek of its own volition. 'You deserve to know how special you are, to be loved...'

She scoffed against his palm, her eyes disbelieving, but he wasn't done...

'You've spent years protecting your family, ensuring you earn an income to support them, giving them a solid shoulder, someone to turn to, but who's been looking out for you, Hannah? Who's protected you?'

Her lips parted, the lost look in her eyes deepening.

'Leon certainly didn't,' he confessed. 'Maybe in the early days, when we were students and you were trying to make ends meet. When it was all about who you knew rather than what you knew, he had your back. But the last few years I've watched the gulf between you grow. He's been so focused on making partner, so riddled with jealousy that we were already there, he's pushed us both away and you'd have seen that if you weren't so blind to it.'

Her eyes narrowed, confusion sparking in their misty depths.

'Don't you think it's time to carve out a new path for yourself, free of him, free of the lie?'

'Our marriage wasn't a lie.'

'It was a lie in all the ways that matter. And now he's taken the choice away from you, the control, and that's what scares you the most.'

'It isn't that simple.'

'It is. When you still had the lie, the marriage, the image you wanted, it was okay—now he's calling the shots instead of you, exposing the truth and you're kicking up a fuss.'

'This isn't a fuss, Brendan, I'm not a child having a paddy.'

'Really? You could have fooled me, Ice.'

'Don't call me that.'

'Why? You earned the name at Oxford and it's never suited you more.'

'Now that I'm practically on my knees begging you to be there for me?'

He choked on the image she painted: Hannah on her knees before him. No. Never going to happen and yet his blood fired with it anyway. He shouldn't be this close to her. It was too much, too easy to stroke the worry lines from her brow, thumb that pout from her full mouth…to dip and kiss…

'You should go.'

He stepped away sharply and she tugged him back. 'No.'

His pulse leapt. 'No?'

'Not until you stop looking at me like that.' Her eyes pierced his.

'Like what?'

'Like—like you hate me.'

'*Hate* you?' He raked an unsteady hand through his hair, walked away and this time she let him. 'I don't *hate* you.'

The word caught in his throat, his voice vibrating around the word. If only he could hate her, had been able to hate her, he wouldn't have spent the last decade torturing himself, a friend and colleague to her and her husband. A triangle he wanted no part of but couldn't escape.

'Are you sure about that?'

His brows drew together as he turned to face her, his eyes locked in hers and drowning ever deeper. 'Of course, I'm sure.'

'Then why have you been so distant?' She placed her whisky on the glass coffee table and stepped towards him. 'I've never needed you more these past two years and you've been pulling further and further away.'

'That's not true.'

Liar, it's called self-preservation and you know it.

She continued towards him, her scent invading his senses, so familiar, so provocative, not that she could know. Not that she had any inkling of just how much he *did* care.

'I don't believe you.'

'Why stay in a loveless marriage for so long, Hannah?' he deflected.

'Because love has the power to destroy you.' She reached up and touched her palm to his cheek, the move as surprising as the heat it sent coursing through his veins. 'You and me, Brendan, we're the same.'

He stared down into her eyes, fought back the wailing storm within. 'No. We're not the same, Hannah.'

His parents might have taught him the heart-break that came from loving someone and witnessing their downfall, but it hadn't prevented him from feeling it for himself. It hadn't prevented him from falling in love with a woman he could never have.

Her lashes lowered and her hand fell away. 'You're right, you're better than me, and I'm sorry I've disappointed you.'

She was already walking away before he woke up to her words and he slammed his glass down. 'No, Ice. Get back here.'

CHAPTER TWO

No, SHE NEEDED to keep moving because if she stopped the tears would fall and she'd already cried enough.

Her heels clipped against his rich wooden floor, their beat resonating with her pulse that had been off the charts from the moment she had touched him. She shouldn't have come here. She shouldn't have brought her problems to his door. It wasn't fair on him, on them, or his previous friendship with her soon-to-be ex-husband.

She swiped at her cheeks, but it was no use. Her surroundings continued to blur, the high-end furnishings, all hard angles and glass, the dark grey sofa and sleek grand piano… The entire room was Brendan all over. Suave. Sophisticated. Cool and controlled.

But he wasn't any of that right now, thanks to her.

'Hannah!'

His fingers wrapped around her wrist and that inexplicable heat raced through her. So wrong but so acute. She shook her head, took another step forward but it failed to land. She was spinning on her heel, her ponytail flicking out.

'Brendan?' It was a gasp, a confused, electrified gasp as she found herself pressed up against his chest.

His eyes blazed above her, his fingers flexing around her wrist crushed between her breasts and his chest—firm, warm and unyielding. He searched her gaze, thick dark lashes flickering over molten chocolate and flecks of amber she'd never noticed before—never let herself get close enough before.

A crease formed between his brows. A dizzying mix of confusion and something far more potent swelling in his dilated depths. Something far too addictive and consuming and vulnerable with it, and it spoke to the very heart of her.

The background music fell away, their ragged breaths taking over, neither speaking nor moving as they struggled for air. As if they'd run a marathon, not crossed a living room.

This was the true reason she never should have come. She'd known she would crumble. She'd known she'd be vulnerable, known that the burning connection between them would come alive in her weakest hour...

And maybe that's why you did come. Maybe you wanted it. Wanted this. Wanted him.

No. She shook her head, fighting her inner voice as she tried to remember what he'd said, what she'd said in return to trigger his desperate move. Because it was desperation, of that she was sure. Brendan was too like her when it came to acting out, showing weakness, emotion of any sort.

'It's okay. You don't need to take it back.' She raised her chin though her voice was soft. 'You're right. I'm cold and calculated and as selfish as they come.'

She would own who she was because she'd actively become that person. She'd had to in order to survive in a world where her parents had played the child and she'd been the responsible one.

There was no denying it suited the lawyer in her too.

He made a sound akin to a growl and it vibrated through his body, caressing her own. '*Yes*, you're calculating. *Yes*, you can be cold. And *yes*, you can be selfish. But there's more to you than that.'

She shook her head, the frenzied ache low in her abdomen making any words impossible.

'You *care*, Hannah. You care deeply.'

She wet her lips, his impassioned words teasing at that place she kept locked away. 'How can you say that?'

'Because I *do* know you. And there's so much more beneath the fine facade. In the name of your family and your clients, you present that front, but it's fuelled by your heart. The day I met you, you spoke of justice, of defending the innocent, protecting the innocent…you talked with such passion and care.'

'The day we met…' That was fifteen years ago—she remembered it all, but to know that he did too… 'You remember?'

'How could I forget? You held the entire room captive.'

Him too; he didn't need to say it for her to know it.

She remembered glimpsing him in the lecture theatre, a tall, dark contrast beside Leon's blond good looks. She recalled the same appreciation in his eyes then, the subtle quirk to his lips… had pondered the spark and swiftly dismissed it. Leon was safe. Her feelings for Leon she could keep contained, keep control of… But Brendan, she'd always known he would threaten more, take more…

Then why are you here, risking it now?

Because she wanted to. She craved his calm, his solidity, his security…but there was security and then there was this overarching pull, the need to reach up on tiptoes and taste those lips that were forbidden. Would always be forbidden.

He was her best friend. Worse, he was her soon-to-be ex's ex–best friend. Did all those exes make it okay?

And what are you even doing contemplating it? You've already lost Leon…do you really want to push Brendan away too?

'I should go.'

'If you must…' Tension pulsed through his frame, his voice as tight as his unyielding grip upon her wrist, her waist. 'But answer me one thing, Hannah.'

'Anything.'

Why did that sound like a plea rather than consent?

And a plea for what exactly…?

'Why come to me?'

She tried to clear the lustful haze clouding up her brain, ease the frantic race to her pulse. 'I already told you.'

'Because you believed I'd understand?'

'I *hoped* you'd understand. You know me better than anyone.'

'Then trust me when I tell you to give him his divorce. Don't fight it.' His eyes lowered to her lips. 'Not because he wants it, but because you should want it too.'

She swallowed past the tightness in her throat, the burn in her chest, the thrum to her lips. He was too close like this, far too close.

'You deserve to find that passion you and Leon lost. You deserve it all and more.'

And what if she told him that passion had never existed? Not on the scale he spoke of, not on the scale she felt right now crushed up against him. Leon and she had gone through the motions, done the expected, a box-ticking exercise in her life plan.

Would Brendan change his mind about her? Would he hate her? Would he realise she really was cold and unfeeling and unworthy of it?

His grip eased, a sudden chill washing over her as air invaded the gap he created between them and she instinctively sought to fill it, to bring him back to her, the confession falling from her lips unbidden…

'You make me feel things, Brendan. Things I shouldn't.'

His eyes flashed, those full lips quirked, but she couldn't stop. Her head was telling her to quit but her heart wanted him to know it all…

'The truth is you're the only person I'm my true self with, the only person I want to speak to when life gets tough, the only person capable of making me feel like everything would be okay. When Leon hit a downward spiral, it was you I would come to, you who'd reassure me. When Mum had her accident, it was you I called to pull me back from the brink, to give me the strength I needed to be there for her and for Jessie…'

She touched her hand to his cheek, marvelling at the way the simple contact fizzed through her. She might crave his security, but she ran from this—the connection that tested the very limits of her control. She'd forced it into a box, clamped the lid on tight over a decade ago and now…now that box was creaking open and she couldn't stop the words that fell from her lips.

'You're the only one who's ever given me that support, that comfort, and you're the only one who's ever made me feel like this...'

His head dipped until their noses almost touched and his whisky-scented breath swept over her lips. 'This?'

She tilted her head back, brought him closer. 'Yes.'

Did she need to put a word to it? No.

He knew. She could see it in the heat of his eyes.

'Does this feel comforting to you?' And then he dragged the lightest of kisses across her mouth and she couldn't breathe, couldn't think. Pandora's box was flying open and her over-sensitised body couldn't care. Couldn't care and craved more.

Had she ever felt this alive? This incredible? All from the gentle brush of someone's lips.

No. Not someone's. Brendan's. This was all Brendan and the power he wielded over her... whether he meant to or not.

'Does it feel reassuring and safe, Hannah?'

No, her brain screamed as pleasure, a twisted heat that had her toes curling in her heels, sent a gasp flying from her lips and he caught it with his kiss, his groan as provocative as his mouth moving over hers.

'Or this?'

He released her wrist and brought her up against him hard. Sparks of delight firing from every point they touched. Immobilising her. Holding her hostage.

She didn't dare breathe for fear it would stop, didn't dare move for fear *he* would stop...but she couldn't prevent her body from leaning in, craving the solid heat of his as she parted her mouth to him.

He groaned low in his throat, his grip tightening as his tongue grazed against hers and her knees threatened to buckle, an erotic shiver rippling through her middle.

'You taste better than I ever imagined.' The breathless rasp to his voice was heady, intoxicating, his need pressing between them so obvious and deepening the reciprocal throb in her core.

And then his words registered. *Imagined.* Had he imagined it? Had he dreamt of it as she had...?

She'd never let herself consciously go there, never let the idea take hold...but her dreams had tortured her, her subconscious finding a way to taunt her with the what if...

She'd been faithful to Leon. Of course, she had. Dreams didn't count.

But this, this was no dream and the aching pull in her abdomen, the tension coiling through her every limb... Her dreams had nothing on the thrilling reality. Of kissing Brendan. Off-limits Brendan. Brendan who'd always made her feel too much. A risk she couldn't take.

But tonight, she was sick of doing things by the

book—the great Hannah Rose book. Guided by her childhood, dictated by her parents whose love had been so fierce it had been ugly. Twisted and unhealthy. An emotion certain to ruin anyone it touched, but not Hannah.

She'd sworn she would never make herself that vulnerable, succumb to anything close. Anything with the power to drive such emotion wasn't to be trusted.

But this…what *was* this? And what was she doing?

Feasting on feelings. Hormones. An irrational attraction that had always been a threat to her status quo…

But she was tired, done with it, done with life almost…until Brendan's kiss.

'I need you.' It came out weak, lost in her inner battle, but it was enough to see him tearing his mouth from hers.

'What are you saying?'

He stared down into her eyes and she couldn't believe how different he was. From the controlled, distant man upon her arrival to the man he was right now, the glint of hope, of need reflected right back at her. How would he look if they came together? Where would his control be then? How would it feel?

Her thighs clenched together, her voice silenced by her own rising need.

'Hannah? Don't tease me, don't—'

She pressed a finger to his lips, held his gaze. She should take it back but even as she thought it she dragged her finger down, cherishing the give of his lip beneath the pressure, the hint of stubble on his chin, his neck, lower still until she reached the first fastened button of his shirt, and with her words she released it. 'I want you.'

His throat bobbed, a moment's hesitation, and then he was kissing her, hard and fast, crushing her to him as all hell broke loose. He tugged her blouse from her skirt as she shoved his shirt from his shoulders, a second's breach as he yanked it over his wrists to toss it aside and then he was back, stripping her blouse with hands as rough as his mouth.

'I want you, too,' he growled. 'But are you sure?'

'I'm done thinking,' she rasped against his lips. 'I just want to feel.'

Their eyes clashed, one beat, two as he sought what he needed in her gaze. 'You and me both.'

And then they were fused together, his hands raking over her, her fingers clawing at his hair, begging for more. She wanted him everywhere all at once, her entire body crying out for his attention.

She jolted when her naked back hit the cool glass of the window, her gasp swallowed by his kiss. When had they moved? Could people see? His penthouse was high above ground level, no one directly opposite, but New York was the city of skyscrapers…and telescopic voyeurs.

'No one can see,' he murmured against her lips, as though he were in her head, reading her thoughts, her wants, her heart's desire. 'It's just you and me, baby.'

You and me, baby.

Something heavy turned over in her chest. Something that made her neck prickle, her pulse skitter. She tried to catch her breath, tried to ignore it, tried to kiss him to forget it but he leaned back, his eyes burning down as he tugged the grip from her hair.

'I've burned to do that for so long—' he forked his fingers through her freed locks, cupped the back of her head '—to see your hair free, to see you free.'

His words were dizzying. Tears that made no sense burned the backs of her eyes and she squeezed them shut, dragged his mouth back to hers. Felt his hands skim the lace edge of her bra and her breath hitched, her body stilled, anticipation pulling her body taut. He slowed his caress, his touch tantalisingly soft. Her breasts heaved, pleading in their beaded state, tingling against the lace. The first sweep of his thumbs across her nipples and she bucked, bit her lip to trap her cry.

His fingers slipped beneath her bra straps, lowering the fabric, exposing her to the cool air and his hot gaze. She arched back, her body pleading for what her voice failed to demand as he trailed his kisses lower. She wrapped one leg around him, seeking to ease the budding ache.

'You smell of heaven and earth and everything in between.'

If anyone else had said it to her, she would have laughed, the sentiment foolish and ridiculous. But from Brendan, for her, laughter was a distant rumble, drowned out by the illicit fire and warmth.

'I'd never put you and poetry together.' Her hands were on his shoulders, her eyes on his as he hovered just above one rose-tipped peak.

'Me neither.' And then he took her into his mouth, and she rocked back with a cry, pleasure all-consuming and driving her to the precipice— too quick to stop, too thrilling to fight.

She clutched his head to her. 'Don't stop. Please don't stop.'

'Believe me, I don't intend to.' His breath caressed her skin, his lips lightly sweeping and she writhed against him, her skirt hitching higher as he smoothed his palm along her thigh. Higher and higher until his thumb teased over the lace of her thong and she clamped her teeth down on her lip, trying to contain the chaos, the insanity, the explosion that was far too close.

'You drive me wild, Hannah. The things I want to do to you, with you...'

She was nodding, panting, her climax continuing to spiral thick and fast.

'Brendan, you're…this…' She couldn't come so soon. She couldn't. But she could feel it as sure as she could feel his teeth tease at her nipple, his fingers slipping beneath the lace into her dampened heat. 'I want you. I want you. I want you…'

The confession was tumbling out of her, nonsensical. She lost sight of what she voiced and what she mentally cried out as her body drew tight, her head flew back and her orgasm took over, tying up her tongue, twisting up her heart—she was in heaven and hell all at once. Delirious with pleasure.

Pleasure that could so readily become an addiction, and in its wake came the icy prickle of fear. Fear she didn't want to let in and so she wrapped herself up in him and all that she could trust. Absorbed his warmth as he lifted her into his arms and cradled her like a child. He carried her to his bedroom, laid her down on his sheets and slowly brought her back to the peak, stripping her of her clothing and his own as she lay there feeling worshipped, treasured, desired.

He pulled a condom from his bedside drawer and sheathed himself, the entire time his eyes locked in hers as if he was afraid she would suddenly disappear, run…

As though he could read her mind, her deep-seated fear, but her body, her heart…they were right where they wanted to be.

He hovered over her, eased her legs apart with

his own, his gaze as soft and as searing as his words. 'Are you sure?'

Her throat closed over, those blasted tears making a return and tying up her tongue. So she did what she could, she reached up, pulled him close enough to brush his nose with her nod. She wrapped her legs around him and drew him to her, but he fought against the pressure.

'Say it, Hannah. I need to hear you say it.'

'I want you.' It came without thought, without fear or doubt. It came because it was the truth and, in that moment, she needed him to know it.

With a groan, he moved, entering her with such control she knew he was taking his time for her. That all this had been about her, and it crushed her even as it warmed her, even as she lifted her mouth to his and nipped his lip with her teeth. Punishing him for his patience, worshipping him for his care.

'I don't need gentle, Brendan. I won't break.'

She forced him onto his back with her words and took what she wanted, what he needed. The carnal heat in his eyes as he watched her move over him, every rock of her hips as she swept her hair back from her face and he caressed her breasts, the groans that he gave… She'd never felt so wild, so desired, so free.

'That's it, Hannah. Feed the passion. Let go. Let go for me.'

And she did… The passion he spoke of, the passion she had run from for so long, she was riding it, engulfed by it. Never had she felt so empowered. Not in the courtroom and never with Leon.

He gripped her thighs, his body pulling taut as her name wrenched from his lips. He launched himself up, his body juddering beneath her as he wrapped his arms around her, held her fast as her own climax claimed her.

They rode the waves together, his head pressed into her shoulder, her fingers in his hair. It was perfect, no pretence, all real, and as their movements slowed, their breaths evening out, the realisation wriggled cold in the pit of her gut, and she breathed in his scent, his warmth, fought it back. It had been too incredible, too out of this world to spoil.

Tomorrow she could think on it. Tomorrow, she could call herself a fool for succumbing to it all.

But for now…maybe she could stay a little longer. Maybe they could share a drink. Find their footing. Work out how they moved on from here—

And you're really thinking on the practical when he's still…?

She shifted over him and he jerked upright, his curse as unexpected as his sudden pallor.

Her fingers stilled, the chill took over. 'What's wrong?'

But she already knew. She could feel the answer slipping between them and read it in his widened gaze.

* * *

'Mum, will you stop fussing?'

Hannah tried to bat away her mother's fingers as she adjusted the veil around her face for the umpteenth time.

'Are you sure this is what you want? You can still change your mind. You don't need to be rushing down the aisle when you have your whole life ahead of you.'

'I hardly call a three-year engagement rushing and I'm thirty. It's a good time for me to get married. Leon's career is taking off, I've made partner...it's the next obvious step.'

'But are you sure you're doing it for the right reasons?'

'What's the right reason, Mum? We're good together, he makes me laugh, he's great with the board and I love that I don't have to worry about finding a date for the many and varied functions we have to attend.'

'And what about love?'

'I love you. I love Jessie. And Leon and I...we love our life together. It works.'

'You make it sound more like a business deal,' Jessie grumbled from beneath her skirts, where she was straightening the layers of tulle.

'And you're only twenty and too wrapped up in those romance novels you read. You've plenty of time to work out for yourself that the love they paint is idealistic at best and dangerous at worst.'

'Hannah!' Her sister appeared above the fabric, her eyes wide. 'How can you say that? On your wedding day of all days?'

But Hannah wasn't looking at Jessie. She was looking at her mother and remembering all the many and varied ways her parents had taught her that love couldn't be trusted.

Not the kind that they both spoke of.

CHAPTER THREE

'WE SHOULD HAVE taken this conversation to the bar...'

Brendan dragged his eyes from the computer screen to take in Simon's presence on the other side of his desk. His friend's grin more bemused than genuine.

'Come on, what gives?'

'What do you mean, what gives?'

'I just told you my sister has called off her engagement and joined a commune and you barely blinked.'

He grimaced, pinching his nose. 'Now that I'd love to see.'

'Simone as a nun? Do you want the convent to burn?'

He laughed as he leaned back in his seat. 'Fair point.'

'So come on, what's going on? You're a workaholic but even by your standards this is getting out of hand. You've been back in London two weeks and you've rarely left the office.'

'And you know that how...?'

'I have my sources.'

'You mean you've been leading my PA astray again.'

Simon shrugged, the spark in his blue eyes telling Brendan all he needed to know. 'She's getting paid to work, not fraternise with my friends.'

Simon chuckled. 'And what if I said she'd been off the clock?'

Brendan held his hand up. 'Enough. I don't need to know any more.'

'Good, because I don't want to talk about me, I want to talk about you. If it's not the hotel chain, which, let's face it, no longer needs so much of your input with your ever-efficient team, it's the extra cases you're picking up and far be it from me to tell you this, but you need to get a life.'

'Now you sound like your brother.' He shoved out of his seat and crossed the office, pulling open the drinks cabinet in the corner.

'Joel? You've spoken to him recently?' Simon nodded as Brendan gestured with a bottle of his finest. 'Isn't he still at your place in Mustique?'

'He is...' Brendan concentrated on pouring the whisky rather than on the guilt he felt at aiding Joel in his quest to avoid the world. 'He was supposed to leave yesterday but there was an incident on the way to the airport. All's fine,' he was quick to add, sensing Simon's sudden worry, 'but he missed his flight out.'

'I bet he did.' His friend raked a weary hand down his face. 'How did he seem to you?'

Brendan lifted his gaze to the Thames, to the lights of Tower Bridge striking out against the darkness, and pondered how best to say it. 'He seemed like Joel. No better, but no worse either.' He crossed the room and handed Simon his drink. 'Life's one big party.'

He huffed. 'Did you mention the meeting in Tokyo?'

'I did.'

'And?'

'It went about as well as you'd expect. He's not ready to return to the family business.'

'He's not ready to return to the family, period.'

Brendan couldn't deny it. 'He just needs time.'

'How much time? Another week, a month, a year…' He blew out his frustration, knowing Brendan couldn't answer that. No one could. 'When's he due to fly back?'

'Imminently.' He dropped back into his seat. 'Hannah's sister is out there.'

'She is? That doesn't sound very wise.'

'He was supposed to vacate before she arrived…'

'Oh.'

'Yeah, oh.'

'I assume you've warned him to leave well alone.'

Brendan grunted. Of course he'd warned Joel. But now his mind was on Hannah, as it seemed to be every hour of every day, and he couldn't clear it. The vision of her that night, their conversation and her rapid exit, the worry…

He'd replayed it over and over in his head. The passion, the intense connection, and then the chill. The methodical way she'd moved into crisis planning, all emotion stripped from her voice as she'd pulled on her clothes. Not once reaching his gaze and then she'd stood in his doorway, Ice through and through, as she told him very clearly: *'It will be okay, Brendan. This is what the morning after pill is designed for. Don't think on it a second more.'* And left.

She'd flown back to London on a separate flight and he'd only caught glimpses of her since. A flash of cool sophistication, her dress and make-up immaculate, her famed poise unaffected, but none of that could conceal the increasing hollowness to her cheeks, her frame worryingly slight.

He wanted to pull her aside and ask if she was okay but all their communication took place via email or their PAs. Arranging her sister's trip to Mustique. Her businesslike gratitude. The odd advice on a case.

No warmth. No connection. They were broken.

'…the convent welcomed her with open arms, you know, she's redesigning their habits as we speak.'

'Huh?' He frowned, his brain playing catch-up as he caught the tail end of what Simon was saying. 'I'm sorry, Si, I'm just…distracted.'

'Tell me something I don't know. Is this the real reason you didn't come to dinner on Sunday? Because you don't normally pass up the opportunity when you're in London.'

He was right; an invite to dinner with the Austin family always took precedence. Ever since they'd welcomed him into the fold as a teen, they'd become as important and as loved as the family he had lost.

'Mum was straight on at me to pay you a visit and check all was okay. And as much as we all worry about Joel, I'm sure he's not the reason for those bags under your eyes and that stray quiff you've got going on there…' Simon twirled a finger in the direction of Brendan's hair as he raked a self-conscious hand through it. 'Yup, that'll be the cause of it right there.'

'Is there anything that passes you by?'

'Can I help it if I'm very observant?'

'Joel's right, you know.'

'Ha, in what way?'

'You are pretty annoying.' Brendan's lips twitched into a half-smile. 'Two years our junior and acting like the elder.'

Simon laughed. 'Hardly. I just care. Joel hit the brink hard—he's still hitting the brink—and I'll be damned if I see you go the same way because you won't lean on us.'

Never going to happen. Brendan had witnessed

Joel at his worst, saved his life in that moment too, and that night had left its mark.

'I'm fine.' His voice was gruff with the past, raw with the present. 'It's nothing I can't handle, at any rate.'

Because he had been handling his feelings for Hannah, he'd been handling them for years.

'And normally I'd believe you, but…'

'It's Hannah.'

Simon's brows lifted. 'And now it makes sense.'

'And what's that supposed to mean?'

Simon considered him for a moment, then threw back his whisky and smacked it down on the desk. 'Come on, I'm getting you out of here, we need a real drink.'

Brendan frowned at the glass in his hand. 'I'll have you know this is—'

'I mean a beer, Brendan, in a pub.' He got to his feet, buttoned up his suit jacket. 'Then we can talk all about Hannah and what's going on with you, man to man. Drink up!'

There was no use arguing. With a wince he threw back his whisky, all appreciation for the drink lost. Giving a silent apology to the Johnnie Walker gods that their Blue Anniversary edition, no less, had been so abused, he got to his feet. 'You Austin men are Neanderthals, I swear.'

'Whatever you say, bro.'

Tugging his jacket off the back of his chair, Brendan slotted his mobile into the pocket and followed Simon to the door. 'You know, next time you want to throw back a drink, warn me first, I can be a little more selective.'

'And where's the fun in that?'

'Remind me again why—'

His phone buzzed with an incoming message and he broke off to pull it out. He checked the screen and his heart stuttered, his jaw clenching shut.

'What is it? You look like you've seen a ghost...'

It took him a moment to register Simon's voice over the ringing in his ears, over the message blaring up at him from Hannah. Simple and disturbing.

We need to talk.

'Or should I be asking *who* is it?'

'It's Hannah.'

It's always Hannah.

His grip around the phone pulsed, his eyes boring into the message.

'The woman's clearly got superhero hearing, wanting to get to you before you have chance to spill all.'

He couldn't even laugh, not with the continuing roll in his gut.

What did it mean? There was a time she would have called him after hours to discuss a complex case, or to see if he was working late too and fancied grabbing a takeaway in the office, but all that had stopped the day he'd gone to her with news of Leon's affairs.

And it had been almost two months since that night in New York. Two months...

He quit thinking and typed back.

I'm just leaving the office, I can call at your apartment within the hour.

Her response was instant.

Not here.

Where?

Your place?

Are you sure that's wise?

He had no idea why he questioned it. It wasn't like his place in New York where he couldn't walk through it without thinking of her being there. Up against the glass. In his bed...the memory alone was enough to heat his veins and aggravate the churn that upped tenfold with her response:

It's less likely to get out.

Less likely that Leon would learn of it, she meant. He raked a hand through his hair, blew out a breath. As far as he knew, the divorce was proceeding, and Leon was taking an extended vacation with his new woman. Whatever Hannah got up to would hardly feature on Leon's radar, but he wasn't about to stick the knife in and say so.

It would be different if Leon knew what had happened between them, of course it would. He'd have plenty to say about it. Hypocritical, yes. Understandable, even more so.

Fine. Seven p.m. I'll sort dinner.

No need.

I insist. You look like you haven't eaten a square meal in too long.

He regretted the message as soon as he'd sent it, regretted it even more as the dots appeared showing she was typing, stopped and started again. He waited and waited, Simon a quiet and unusually patient third wheel.

Then…

There really is no response to that. Not one I'd type anyway.

His mouth quirked at the hint of fire. It was still in there somewhere. They weren't entirely broken…yet.

There is. You say thank you. Any special requests?

Dino's?

The flicker of a smile touched his lips. Dino's pizza, they hadn't had one in years…pizza had been traded in for high-end sushi, soba noodles, fancy dishes that looked just as good in a tray as they would on a plate. Cleaner. Leaner. Healthier.

But pizza took them back in time, to happier times…was that a good sign? Was this a truce? A reset, even?

The usual?

Please.

Panic easing a little, he gave Simon an apologetic grin. 'Sorry, mate, I'm going to have to take a rain check on that beer.'

Simon cocked a one-sided grin that smacked of his older brother. 'So long as it keeps that smile on your face I can deal. I fly to Tokyo on Monday. If you can get Joel to join me, I'll not only take you up on the rain check, I'll even pay.'

Brendan laughed. 'You're on.'

His phone buzzed, then buzzed again…and again.

Frowning, he looked back at the screen.

Extra jalapeños. And olives. Hold the garlic.

He gave the smallest shake of his head. Bemused. Since when had…?

And pineapple, please.

As he was saying, since when had Hannah been so indecisive? And *pineapple*? That was sacrilege. But he typed back.

As you wish x

And then swiftly deleted the 'x'.
This was a reset. Not a redo!

Hannah couldn't stop twisting her fingers together, an annoying habit she'd developed since she'd taken the dreaded test and been forced to face reality. She was pregnant. Pregnant!

Going through a divorce at thirty-eight was bad enough. To be going through a divorce and pregnant by her best friend was something else!

The trip to her GP the day after had been humiliating. She'd felt like a naughty schoolgirl caught doing something she shouldn't. And now… now she would be the woman who'd not only slept with someone other than her husband, but she'd also got pregnant by him too.

Pregnant by her once best friend and current colleague.

They'd be the talk of the firm.

They'd be—

The lift doors opened. Brendan's city loft apartment stretched out before her and there he was—dark hair, dark eyes, dark clothes, and a razor-sharp five-o'clock shadow. Her heart gave an involuntary leap as her fingers continued their tango.

'Hannah.'

She gripped the disobedient digits tight and her lips parted but no words would come.

Why did her name suddenly sound so different when he said it? Was her mind inserting 'baby' where it didn't belong? The phantom feel of that mouth sweeping over her own...

She wet her lips though it was no use, her mouth was bone dry, her eyes wide as she drank him in. She hadn't looked at him properly since that night and her eyes were too eager, her heart too as it pulsed with the knowledge of what she had to tell him.

She pressed her palm to her stomach, gave a whispered, 'Hi.'

'You'd best come in before the doors close.'

Was it her imagination, or did he sound hoarse? Gruff? Was he struggling with this reunion as much as she was? Did he suspect what she had to say?

He stepped towards her and she came alive, moving before he could touch her.

'I'm sorry to interrupt your Friday.' Her eyes darted about the room, anywhere but him.

'You didn't.'

She flicked him a weak smile—did he always look so good in jeans? Jeans and a simple sweatshirt. Or was it enhanced by the fact she hadn't let herself look at him in so long? Scared that she'd give herself away, give them away. Soon she wouldn't have a choice but to give them both away, her stomach would do it for her.

She almost squeaked with the thought and racked her brain for something easy to say. Something conversational. Non-confrontational. 'I'd forgotten how different this apartment is.'

'Are we really doing the whole small talk?' He must have read something worrying in her face because he immediately acquiesced. 'Different from what?'

She swallowed. 'Your place in New York.'

She wasn't lying. She had forgotten. Had it really been that long since she'd been here? Probably. Leon had been with her the last time. They'd had dinner in his kitchen, joked about work, about life… There'd been an edge to Brendan then though, she'd sensed it, confronted Leon about it too and been told the lie. *Everything's fine.*

What had been the problem that night? The

deterioration of their friendship or had Brendan known of Leon's affairs as early as then?

'Do you prefer it?' Brendan pulled her back to the present, thankfully sticking with her *safe* conversation.

'I like them both for different reasons.' Again, no lie. It was warm here, industrial yet cosy. The exposed redbrick walls with their huge arching windows crossed by steel. The high ceiling softened by the exposed beams and honey oak floor. Another grand piano took up one corner of the living space—it struck her then that she hadn't heard him play in a long time. While in the other, a light grey sofa dominated, curving around a low-slung coffee table that sported the all-important pizza boxes.

Their scent drifted across the room and her stomach grumbled.

'Come on, you need to eat.'

She did, though she didn't think she could get any food past the confession choking up her throat. 'We should talk first.'

'I guess it's too much to hope that you're here to discuss Jessie's unexpected roommate in Mustique?'

She gave a gentle scoff. No, she didn't need to be reminded of that on top of everything else. 'It's hardly the best news.'

'I know it's not ideal but he'll hopefully be gone soon.'

'And if he's not?'

'He really isn't as bad as the media make out.'

'Are you sure about that?' She wanted to believe him, but Joel was a man at the end of the day and her sister was an attractive, single redhead with a vulnerable heart and a trusting smile.

'He's assured me he's on best behaviour.'

'And you believe him?'

'Until he gives me cause to think otherwise.'

She studied him a second longer and nodded. 'Okay. I trust you.'

'Good. And on the subject of Jessie, how did she take the news?'

'News?'

'Of you and Leon? The divorce?'

She stared back at him.

'You *have* told Jessie?'

She swallowed. 'Not yet—' his eyes widened and she hurried to add '—but I will! I just want her to have this holiday, first. To enjoy the break and find herself again. I need her to be in a better place before I offload my own troubles on her.'

'Right, whatever you say...'

'I do.'

Silence as they studied one another, questioned, doubted...did he not believe her?

'I guess that brings us to the real reason you're here then... If you're worried about Leon finding out, he won't hear it from me. I swear to you.'

She clenched her jaw, her body turning rigid

save for her fingers that started their merry dance again. His eyes rested on the move and she clutched them together. 'Do you know what? I've changed my mind. Dino's is much better hot.'

'But you said you wanted to talk first.'

'And like I said, I've changed my mind.'

'It can't be as bad as all that, just say it, whatever it is, get it off your chest.'

She couldn't. Because it *was* as bad as all that. In fact, it was worse. This was the kind of secret no one could keep—in a few weeks it would be obvious to all and sundry.

'You better sit down before you fall down.'

Did she really look that bad?

He gestured to the sofa and she moved with him, sitting a safe distance away. Close enough to reach the pizza but far enough away not to reach him. Maybe she should have refused dinner altogether. Food and this conversation didn't mix.

He took up the bottle of wine she hadn't noticed previously and offered it to her.

Her cheeks warmed, her eyes once again averted. 'Not for me.'

'Do you mind if I…?'

She shook her head, watching the bottle as he poured. Was she projecting, or was there a tremor to his hand?

'I don't have a lot of soft drinks in. I can do orange juice, tonic—'

'A tap water's fine.' And it gave her chance to

take in air without his scent, gave her space to think while he fetched it.

He nodded, the grave look in his eye enough to have the confession reach her tongue but she forced it back and watched him go. Counted to ten. At least let him sit back down first...

'You don't look so well,' he said on his return, offering out the glass. 'I'm worried about you.'

'It's been a weird few weeks.'

And then some...

'Weird as in not eating weird?'

'We're back to commenting on my waistline, are we?'

He dropped down beside her, closer than she'd like. Closer than her body could tolerate without her skin prickling to life, craving his proximity.

'No insult intended, more that I'm sorry if what happened between us has been preying on your mind, if the divorce has been getting to you, too. I know you and Leon were—*are* technically still married and I shouldn't have crossed that line.'

She sipped at her water. 'As the saying goes, it takes two to—' she almost said make a baby and blurted '—tango.'

'True.'

'And you don't owe me an apology. If anything, I owe you one. You tried to do right by me a long time ago and I shut you out.'

'We shut each other out.'

The vehemence in his words surprised her, his

willingness to take responsibility for his part too. But why should it when Brendan had always been good, kind, compassionate…? Everything Leon hadn't been.

She tried to ignore the pressure behind her ribs, the foreign ache she couldn't get a handle on, and focus on what mattered. The here and now, not the past, and not the marked differences between the two men.

Brendan wasn't her partner, her lover, her husband—he was her friend and the father of her unborn child. They needed to draw a line under what had happened and move forward.

Make plans, arrangements that would protect them both and, above all, their unborn child. She didn't even know where to begin when it came to motherhood, it had never been on her radar, and that in itself was terrifying.

Terrifying but maybe a little less so once Brendan knew… Brendan, who always seemed to know what to do, what to say…

'Look, Han, I'm—'

'I'm pregnant.'

CHAPTER FOUR

SHE'S PREGNANT. We're pregnant!

The room seemed to shift, or was it simply the speed with which his blood seemed to drain from his entire body…?

'You're—' there was no sound to his voice, nothing but air '—you're pregnant?'

She rolled her shoulders back as regal as a queen and nodded.

'It's yours, in case you're wondering.'

This couldn't be happening. Really, truly, not on the cards, not ever. The whirring in his ears built as his brain raced. He'd come to terms with the fact that she would never be his, written that one night off as an epic mistake that had only solidified what he'd always known. The way she'd run from him, avoided him…

And now she was here telling him they were to be inexorably tied together, for ever. Parents to a child. An innocent little bundle born of that one night…

He'd never envisaged being a father. He'd only ever had a fleeting fantasy of anything close and that had been with Hannah. Hannah who would never truly belong to anyone but herself.

Her heart was reserved for her family and her work. Not even Leon had really claimed a piece of it and she'd been married to him for eight years, together fifteen. Fifteen!

But now she was pregnant and not by Leon—by him!

It couldn't be true and yet, she would never lie. Creative with the truth in the name of the law, sure, but never lie.

'Brendan, say something, please.'

'I thought—I thought you went to see the doctor. The morning after, you said you'd go and…'

'And I did.'

'You got the pill?'

'I did. But apparently, it's not infallible…'

'Not infallible?'

'There's a five per cent failure rate.'

'And we're a failure?'

She choked on an uncomfortable laugh. 'Not how I'd like to put it, but yes, I guess.'

He wanted to press pause, take a moment to clear his mind because his brain was getting dangerously carried away, painting a future of a picture-perfect family. Him. Her. Their child. The image so clear it was almost tangible, urging him to reach out and grasp it before the reality of their situation took over. The reality of who this woman was and what this wasn't took over.

'I know it's a shock and hard to believe, but it's true.'

Of all the women he knew, this was Hannah. Hannah Rose. She'd never taken Leon's name because her name was who she was professionally and personally. Independent and fierce with it. When she'd made partner, she'd earned the mantle of the youngest female to reach such heights within the firm. She hadn't got there by having a life outside work.

She'd got there by being driven, putting her job first, living and breathing it.

Children had never been a part of that plan. Brendan knew it. Leon had bemoaned the fact often enough. He'd never been sure whether Leon's problem came down to his jealousy— vying for his wife's attention over work or having a wife who out-earned him—or if it had been a genuine desire to become a family man himself. Whatever the case, it didn't change the fact that Hannah had never wanted kids.

'What do you want to do?'

She balked, an emotion chasing across her face that he couldn't catch. 'What do you mean, what do I want to do?'

'I mean, about the baby.'

He sensed a fuse blowing behind her eyes, his shoulders lifting as he prepared to do battle. He'd played this so wrong, but he didn't know where else to start.

'I know you mean about the baby. But I was hoping you were asking the question in terms of arrangements—financial, practical, *physical* solutions to how we move forward co-parenting, but you're asking if I want to keep it, aren't you?'

Her hand covered her stomach in a protective gesture that had something twisting inside his chest and he couldn't tear his eyes from where it rested. And that was when he realised it wasn't just the hollowness to her cheeks, the slightness to her frame that had changed. She no longer wore her rings. Leon's rings. The hand over her stomach, bare.

The symbolism served to intensify the chaos inside. There were so many things he wanted to do, wanted to say, but none of it would come out right. No matter which way he tried to phrase it.

He swallowed it all down and he wished he could walk her out and welcome her back in, start again, but it was too late for that.

Some reset.

'Brendan, answer me?'

His eyes flitted back to hers, which were wide with feeling, vulnerable too. 'Is that really such a surprise, Hannah?' His body slumped with his honesty. 'You live for your career. You always have done.'

Her carefully manicured brows drew together. 'I live for my family first.'

'Financially that might be so, but physically...?'

'Financial support *is* what my family required for years, it's what kept a roof over their heads when the money from my no-good father stopped, it's what put food on the table when Mum struggled to hold down a job and it got my sister through university. It's what paid for the extra care my mother needed after her accident, it paid to modify the family home so she could return to it, it covered my sister's loss of income so she could care for her...'

'I know.'

'Do you? Because from where I'm sitting, you're forgetting that some of us weren't so lucky to be born into money, Brendan.'

'That's not...' He raked a hand through his hair. 'I wasn't trying to have a go. I was trying to explain.'

'Whatever your point, I've always had one eye on Jessie. *Always.*' She was so emphatic and the vulnerability in her glittering greys intensified with each word, her chin tilting up. 'Just because a baby was never part of my plan it doesn't mean I can't make room for them too.'

And who was she trying to convince? Herself or him?

'But a baby, Hannah?' He held his hands out. 'What do we know of that responsibility? We're not talking about something you can just drop at day care and forget about. We're talking about a lifetime of responsibility. A dependant who needs to be loved, cherished and cared for.'

'And you don't think I'm up to the challenge?'

'It's not a challenge, Hannah. It's a child!'

The room fell silent, and he couldn't look at her any more. His eyes scanned the room, seeking familiarity, comfort, a calm that didn't exist. His parents might have been fairly absent from his life, but he'd never once doubted their love for one another or for him. He remembered the sense of security that gave, the importance of it and how it had felt the day it had been ripped away.

'Scared you'll have to give up your flash apartments?'

'What?' His eyes snapped back to hers, his frown etched painfully into his face. 'You think that's what I'm thinking?'

'Well, I hardly think the feature wine display is the safest of climbing walls.' She gestured to the cast-iron unit that ran half the length of the dining area, bottle upon bottle resting in its frame. 'All the glass and sharp corners too and those stairs with all the gaps…' Her attention shifted to the twisting staircase that led to the mezzanine floor. 'And don't get me started on your car. Or rather, cars plural. You'll need to rethink that collection, or add to it…'

'Stop it.'

'Stop what?'

'Projecting, deflecting, whatever this stream of

consciousness is. And you know my apartments are no worse than yours, nor my cars for that matter.'

'Yes, but your reaction has been less than encouraging.'

'And just how long have you had to come to terms with this?'

'A week, a little more if you count the symptoms.'

'The symptoms?'

'The lack of period, the sickness, the dizziness, the weight loss… Do you really need me to go on?'

He knew she was fighting him, fighting this, that the fire in her words came from her own fear, her own shock, and he kept his voice soft.

'And you're telling me it didn't knock you for six, Hannah, that you didn't go into some kind of freefall when you saw that test result?'

She didn't answer.

'Just give me some time to take it in.'

'Well, while you're taking your time, I'm going to start making plans…whether they include you or not. I didn't come here to force my decision on you. I'd hoped you would be involved. I grew up with a father who was a drunk, an abuser, a man who believed love was an excuse to lash out and I was far happier when he was gone.'

His gut twisted. 'Are you saying that could be me?'

'No, God no. But I'm saying I did just fine without him and, if necessary, our child will too. I'm saying you can choose to be involved or you can go free. I won't force this child on you, no more than I would give them up.'

She stood and started heading for the door.

'Where are you going?'

'I'm giving you the space you need to take it in.'

He had to fight the roaring sensation within, the very idea of her walking out of his home chilling him to the bone and making him want to race after her.

'I don't want you to leave, Hannah.' He forced himself to stay steady as he came up behind her. 'I want you to stay. I want us to talk about this.'

She stilled but didn't turn and he took hold of her wrist, encouraged her back.

'Please...'

Slowly, she turned and the emotion in her gaze compounded his own. 'You think I care more about all of this—' he waved his other hand at his surroundings '—than our potential child?'

He searched her gaze, beseeching her to see the truth in his.

'There's no potential about it,' she whispered, tugging her wrist from his grip. 'I'm having this baby, Brendan.'

'I know, but you're thirty-eight, Hannah.'

'And?' She wrapped her arms around her middle, her frown confused.

'You need to understand that it's not without its risks, especially at this early a stage.'

She paled beneath her make-up, her lips parting with the smallest gasp, and he wanted to suck the words back in, stamp on them hard. 'Suddenly the expert, are we?'

'You'd be surprised.'

'Really? Been pregnant before, have we?'

He stared back at her, knowing what he had to tell her and not wanting to all the same. The suspicion that for all she was sharp, intelligent, a first-class lawyer…when it came to pregnancy, she might as well be clueless.

He broke away, heading for his wine glass and changing his mind just as quickly. If she couldn't drink, he wouldn't. Instead he turned back to face her, his explanation falling from his lips, 'My parents didn't start trying for a family until much later in life…'

'Keep on with the age thing and this conversation will be over sooner than you think.'

'It is about the age thing.'

'Then explain it faster.'

'Give a guy a chance…'

A hint of colour returned to her cheeks as she gave a brisk nod. A concession, at last, and he breathed the smallest sigh of relief.

'They were always so busy with work, all the travel and living the life…according to my late aunt Mags, I was their sixth pregnancy, and my mother was forty-two when she had me. They were going to give up. It had cost them so much emotionally that they couldn't bear going through it again. Mum had got the decorators in, ripped apart the nursery. It was still in a state of flux the day I was born, five weeks early but alive and kicking.'

She'd gone so very still, if not for the slightest shift to her chest, he'd think she'd given up breathing too. He took a tentative step towards her. 'You haven't researched this at all, have you?'

She was an incredible lawyer, capable of absorbing information like a sponge, researching until the eleventh hour on a case to get what she needed, but when it came to her own pregnancy...

'Have you even seen a doctor, a midwife?'

'Women have babies all the time, Brendan—' the words were a whisper '—and half of them don't live a life as sound as mine. They don't have any issues carrying a baby to term.'

'Have you seen someone, Han?'

'No.'

'Then you need to make that appointment.'

'And I will.'

'When?'

'I don't know, when I get into the office Monday.'

'There must be private clinics who will see you on a Saturday.'

'Nothing's going to change between now and Monday, Brendan.'

He told himself to chill. Knew his own worry would only increase hers. 'You promise?'

She blew out a breath. 'I promise. No more

denial. Coming here was about me being honest with myself as much as you. This is happening whether we like—whether we planned it or not.'

Whether we like it or not.

That was what she'd intended to say. And he couldn't blame her. Still, he had the very real feeling of his heart shrinking in his chest and, reaching out, he took her hand in his. Grateful that she didn't flinch, didn't move away...

'It's going to be okay, Hannah. Whatever happens, it'll be okay.' She nodded, the sudden swell of tears in her eyes crushing him so completely. 'I swear to you, Hannah.'

'I'm sorry, Brendan.' She swiped at an escaped tear. 'I'm sorry that your parents went through all they did. I'm sorry I'm bringing this to your door now. I'm sorry I came to you in New York and—and—'

'Hannah, stop.' Gently, he squeezed her fingers. 'I don't need you to say you're sorry. I need you to be all right. I need you and our baby to be all right.' It came out gruff, throttled with emotion. 'You're not on your own, okay? You have me, and we'll get through this together.'

Together. Him and Hannah. The only woman he had ever loved, and the child she now carried. In that moment, he had everything he could ever want and the fragility of it was suffocating.

'It's time you let someone take care of you for a change, Ice.'

* * *

'You think she's too good for me, don't you?'

Leon grinned at him through the mirror as he tightened his bow tie and Brendan looked out of the window. Pretended to be more interested in the wedding preparations under way in his hotel's grounds, the staff milling about with drinks for the arriving guests...

'Come on. You're my best man. If anyone can be straight with me, it's you.'

Brendan shoved his hands deeper into his pockets. 'As you so aptly put it, I'm your best man, and today is your wedding day. What kind of insensitive idiot do you take me for?'

'The kind that's been in love with my girl since the day you met.'

Brendan's head snapped around, surprise and panic immobilising his tongue as the blood drained from his face.

'Hey, don't look so grey, bud...'

Leon rolled his shoulders back, adjusted his jacket and then, as if deciding he was satisfied with his reflection, turned to face him.

'I've known for a long time and it's okay. I'm fine with it. To be honest, it's kind of a compliment, don't you think?'

Brendan choked back the slick layer of saliva clinging to his throat. 'If you thought I was in love with her, why not have it out with me years ago?'

'And where would be the fun in that? No, no...'

Leon clamped a hand on his shoulder, his grin as open and carefree as ever. 'Besides, you can get anyone you want with your wealth and status. I don't need to worry about you running off with my girl, do I?'

'No.'

To Brendan's ears it felt like a lie. To Leon's it must sound enough.

'Good.' He thumped him on the back and headed for the door. 'Now, let's get this party started! I have it on good authority that the boss of this hotel—i.e. you—has ordered in the best champagne, and I want to make sure I get a look-in.'

Brendan was slow to follow him out, struggling to keep a check on reality. Had that just happened? Had Leon truly accused him of being hot on his girl? No, not hot...worse. In love. And if Leon knew, did Hannah suspect it too?

And what does it matter? They're your best friends and they're getting married. From this day forth it would be a sealed deal...

Leon and Hannah.

No more wondering. No more hoping.

Maybe he could then move on with his life and draw a line under those ancient feelings that he had no right possessing.

CHAPTER FIVE

'I DON'T NEED anyone to take care of me, Brendan,' she blustered. 'I'm more than capable of taking care of me and this child.'

The words left her, strong and unwavering, but inside she was stamping out the rising doubt, the panic, the urge to step closer. To lean into him and have him hold her, to close her eyes and empty out her head, to let him do just as he said—take care of her.

And she knew he would. She knew he'd do anything for her. And the realisation made her want to bolt.

She'd never been dependent on another, never needed someone to hold her hand, to make her feel strong enough, capable enough…

She'd always got there on her own.

Always.

But what did she know about being a mother? What did she know about loving another so wholly and unconditionally? Other than her mother and her sister, she'd closed herself off to that kind of attachment long ago.

'Come on, you need to eat.'

It was so off topic, his suggestion so very normal, it took her too long to react.

'Han, come on…'

He encouraged her back to the sofa and she went, still uncertain, still wary. 'I'm not sure I have much appetite left.'

'Even for Dino's… Dino's with all that weird crap you made me add?'

The flicker of a smile touched her lips, her gratitude to him for at least trying to bring back some normality, some light-heartedness too. 'That weird crap, as you so nicely put it, is just another symptom.'

He lifted the lid on the top pizza box and her stomach came alive, growling in response to the subtle scent that wafted up.

'In that case, forget I said anything.' He sat down beside her. 'My lips are sealed.'

She gave a soft laugh and reached for a piece. 'I hope not, because you'll have a tough time eating if you can't open that mouth of yours.'

And she shouldn't have said it, because now her eyes were trained on those lips and her memory was quick to fire—evocative images coming to life. Of him trailing kisses from her lips to her throat and lower still…

She snapped her eyes away, filling her mouth with pizza as she sought to drown out her erogenous zones with her tastebuds.

And it was delicious, mouth-wateringly so…but

trying to swallow when everything below neck level seemed to be in a heightened state of awareness for him was another battle entirely.

'Everything okay?' He eyed her, his gaze far too astute and far too close. 'You look a little pink in the cheeks.'

'Another symptom,' she blurted. Maybe she could fall back on that excuse every time the need arose…

'Hot flushes? I thought they came later…'

'Let's get one thing straight, Brendan. I'm the woman carrying the child. If I say I'm feeling something, you nod and offer support.'

He chuckled, his eyes dancing, their old camaraderie easing to the fore. 'I can do that.'

'Good. Now eat, because this is bordering on cold and no one wants a—'

'Cold Dino's,' he finished for her, doing as she asked and freeing her to focus on eating her bodyweight in pizza. Though in reality she could scarce manage half…another *genuine* side effect of pregnancy. And as she pushed the box aside, Brendan frowned at the food remaining.

'Not up to par today?'

'Not at all, it's lovely. I just can't manage any more.'

His frown deepened. 'I'm sure you're meant to be eating for two.'

'And as I already told you—' she took up her glass and leaned back into the sofa, welcoming its cushiony softness '—I'm the one whose pregnant so…'

His frown didn't ease. 'But you're losing weight, Han, and you didn't have weight to lose.'

'At least it'll hide the bump a bit longer and forestall the office gossip.'

He cursed and she gave him a weak smile. 'Only just thinking of that now?'

He combed a hand through his hair, stared at the pizza slice that had been halfway to his mouth. 'How do you want to handle it?'

She pondered it for a moment and let him take a bite, waiting for him to swallow before saying, 'I want to avoid it for as long as possible. I'll have to tell HR of course, but that'll be confidential. Then when I can't avoid it any longer, we'll be honest with people.'

'You mean tell them that you're pregnant *and* that I'm the father?'

'Yes. There's no point beating around the bush, they'll find out eventually and I'd rather we controlled the dialogue from the start.'

'Agreed. And you're okay with that?'

No, she wasn't okay. She was terrified. She'd spent so many years projecting perfection, but this wasn't something any perfect facade could hide. There were no other options. None that she would take at any rate. 'I can't see any other way forward.'

'No.' He sank back into the sofa beside her,

his eyes on the dark world beyond the glass. 'Me neither.'

She covered her stomach with her palm, remembering his cautionary tale, what his parents had been through at a similar age…

'Who knows?' Her gut rolled. 'We may be worrying about nothing.'

'No, I think the gossip mill will be rife—you know what Sara's like. For a paralegal I don't know how she gets any work done. And don't get me started on Jonathan. Every time I see him, he's—' He broke off, his eyes resting on her palm. 'That's not what you meant, is it?'

It came out tight and she shook her head, those blasted tears returning—another frustrating side effect, it would seem.

'I'm so sorry, Hannah, I never should have said anything.'

And before she could stop him, he was pulling her into his chest, his chin resting above her head, and he smelled so good, felt so good, so warm and comforting and reassuring and for the first time in too long she just sagged.

Sagged and let the worries set in, let the tears fall and he said nothing, only rocked her, soothed her, stroked her hair in a way that no one else had ever done.

'This is becoming something of a habit, I'm afraid…' She sniffed. She was trying to tease while being honest. She never sobbed, not in public, not alone, not until that night in his apartment when he'd opened the door to her and she'd been so lost over her life as a whole that she'd crumbled.

And here she was again…lost, pregnant, and sobbing on the same shoulder.

Was it possible that Brendan was her Achilles heel? The only one that could make her feel like this. Make her feel safe to let go like this. She scrubbed at her face with the back of her hand, swiping away the tears that wouldn't stop.

'It's healthy to have a good cry, Han. You shouldn't fight it.'

'Oh, really…' She pressed away from him, daring to look him in the face even though she feared she was a hot, snotty mess. 'And when was the last time you bawled your eyes out?'

He stared back at her, unblinking. 'The night I lost my mother.'

The very air stilled. His raw honesty cutting through the heart of her.

'I'm so sorry, Brendan.'

She tried to sit up straight but he pulled her back. 'Oh, no, you don't, you stay right there.'

She relented but her head was too alive with questions and guilt, her own tears forgotten in the age-old wound she'd unintentionally opened. 'I'm sorry, I shouldn't have said that. No one wants to remember when they last sobbed. I didn't think.'

He gave the slightest shrug. 'It was over twenty years ago. Ancient history.'

'That may be but don't dismiss it like it's nothing. That's my trick, not yours.'

His chuckle rumbled through her, edged with emotion. 'I think we both possess that tool in our arsenal.'

She gave a sad smile. 'I guess that's true.'

How did Brendan do it? Manage to make her feel almost normal and not the heartless freak many accused her of being… Leon included.

'It may be ancient history, but it's shaped your entire life… Leon told me it's why you went into criminal law.'

'Did he, now?' His fingers paused in her hair, his voice a low murmur. 'Had quite the conversation about me?'

'Don't let it go to your head.' She tried for a tease. '*Everyone* talked about you.'

A tight chuckle. 'How can I not let that go to my head?'

'You were something of an anomaly. There we were busting our arses because we had to if we wanted good careers, good money. And you, you were the heir to millions in an industry so far removed from the field you were studying. It didn't make sense to many.'

'But it made sense to you?'

She looked up at him, felt the pang of his past deep in her chest. 'Not just me, a lot of the press had it right, too.'

'Wonders never cease, hey?'

'It's admirable, Brendan. I did it because it was the career that interested me most and paid the best. It gave me and my family security. You did it because you wanted to protect people like your father.'

He shifted against the sofa. 'Your motivation was no less admirable, Han. You did it for family, I did it for family. When the law failed my father, convicting him when he was innocent, it ruined his reputation, his marriage…by the time they realised their mistake it was too late. The damage had been done. He was so broken, he was dead within the year and Mum shortly after.'

'Do you think she died from a broken heart?'

He frowned down at her. 'You believe in that?'

'I don't know…it happens often enough for it to have been given a name though. They call it the widowhood effect.'

'How delightful…'

'Delightful and reason enough not to fall in love, right?'

He murmured something nonsensical.

'What was that?'

'I'm not so sure I believe it. Dad was half the man he was before he went to prison, he was ten years older than Mum and his heart had never been the best. Mum was only fifty-five. I think her death had more to do with the fact that when her friends turned their backs on her with Dad's conviction, she turned to gin.'

She snuggled in closer, wanting to bring him comfort while easing the chill spreading within her too. 'Being accused of what your father had can't have been easy for her.'

'No. But she believed him. Getting to the heights they had was never without the risks. The conspiracy theories, the gossip…it was hard. Dad was an advocate for equality between men and women long before it became fashionable. He cared. I guess that made him an interesting target for sexual misconduct.'

'Do you remember much of it?'

He gave a bitter laugh. 'When you're at boarding school and the papers are full of it, it quickly finds a way into your social circle. I got off lightly. They ostracised me, all but Leon and the Austins. Natasha, Joel's mum, she tried to help. She tried to be there for my mother but the humiliation was too much. I don't know whether it was the pity she couldn't stand, or the fear that Natasha would somehow be tainted by association, but she struggled to lean on them.'

'Gin doesn't judge.' Hannah got that. Her mother had often turned to the bottle. Even when she knew what it had done to their father, it still found its way into their life. And even Hannah herself would come home after a hard day at work and pour a glass of wine before thinking twice. She hadn't since she'd learned she was pregnant, but it didn't mean she didn't miss it. There was a lesson there if she was willing to acknowledge it.

'No, it doesn't. And I was away with school, there wasn't anyone to open her eyes to the amount she was drinking. The household staff tried and one by one she got rid of them. She claimed they were an expense we no longer needed to indulge in, but in hindsight, I realised the truth.'

'I'm sorry,' she said, her heart breaking for the boy he had been and the man without a family now.

He shrugged. 'We can't change the past.'

'Only the future…'

The future that suddenly looked so very different. She stroked her fingers over her abdomen that showed no sign of the life beneath. Was this really happening? Her and Brendan having a baby? She tried to visualise it, tried to imagine him holding their child, a boy just like him. Dark eyes, dark hair, pudgy hands…

And the damn tears pricked as her heart fluttered inside her chest.

He'd be a good father, of that she was sure.

As for her…

It wasn't that she was broken. She felt things. She just didn't express them as others did. She could learn though, couldn't she? She'd learned to hide her feelings, she could unlearn it for her baby, couldn't she?

Was it that simple?

She couldn't help the doubt. The worry that she wouldn't be enough. That her cold, heartless persona would prevent her bonding with her baby. Was that where a nanny could come in? Filling in for her by providing the love and affection she would struggle to express? Her stomach twisted, her heart too.

'Are you okay?' His arm pulsed around her and she swallowed, burying herself into him, her mind drifting, her eyes closing. Lord, she was tired. So very tired. When was the last time she had slept properly? The last time she had fallen asleep before midnight as the voices in her head, her inner critic, failed to quit.

'Hannah?'

'I'm okay…just tired. I've not been sleeping very well.'

'That makes two of us.'

'I should leave you in peace.' She went to rise up but he encouraged her back against him…and the lure of his deliciously warm, sweatshirt-soft, masculine-scented chest was too much to resist.

'Just rest. It's still early, Han. The world will still be turning when I'm ready to kick you out.'

She gave a soft laugh, succumbing to the lull of him, the rhythmic beat of his heart beneath her ear, his hand stroking her hair. It was okay to close her eyes, relax for a moment, wasn't it?

Just because he felt this good, didn't make it bad?

It didn't mean anything more.

'Stop thinking.'

He kissed the top of her head and her pulse gave the tiniest leap. If she'd been awake enough, alert enough it would have been her signal to move, instead she cosied down deeper and gave a sleepy scoff. 'You think you know me so well...'

'That's because I do.'

Her heart stuttered in her chest. He wasn't wrong. He *did* know her. He knew her better than anyone and he hadn't run from her, he wasn't afraid of her, he didn't hate her.

Her lips curved up as she drifted on the blissful road to sleep...

'What did I do to deserve a friend like you?'

'Mum! Mum!'

Hannah raced through the house—where was everyone?

'I got the job! They say I can start next Friday after school!'

She took the stairs two at a time.

'Mum!'

There was a sniff from her mother's room and her step faltered.

'Mum...?'

Her voice was softer now, excitement giving way to fear.

She eased open her mother's door. 'Mum?'

She spied her crumpled form on the floor at the end of the bed.

'Oh, Mum!'

She raced to her side, wrapped an arm around her shoulders as she sank down beside her.

'What's happened?'

Her mother shivered in her hold. 'Your father came by...' She sniffed, swiping the back of her hand across her tear-stained face. 'He heard about some guy in The Crown talking to me the other night. Wanted to know who he was...what he wanted.'

'I thought you weren't going to...?'

Her voice trailed off as her mother turned to her, one eye already swollen and bloodshot.

'Oh, Mum.' Hannah pulled her mother to her chest, rocked her as she sobbed. 'I thought you weren't going to let him in again.'

'He was upset...the neighbours were looking...'

'But this has to stop, Mum. You need to call the police. Get him dealt with.'

'I will. I will...'

Hannah wanted to believe her, she really did, but how many times had this happened? How many times had she promised?

'Where's Jessie?'

'I gave her the headphones...stuck a movie on in her room...'

Hannah pressed a kiss to her hair. 'I'll go and check on her. You freshen up, and then we're going to the police station.'

'Now? I can't... I'm a mess.'

'We're catching the bus and we're doing it today.'

'But—'

'No buts, Mum. We need to put a stop to this. To him.'

'I know. I know.' Her mother wrapped her arms around her, tucked her head beneath Hannah's chin. 'You're right. Of course, you're right. You're always right. What would I do without you? You're such a good girl. Such a good daughter and sister. You take such good care of us.'

'Always, Mum. Always...'

CHAPTER SIX

THE COFFEE MACHINE GURGLED, announcing the end of the brew, and Brendan grabbed an oversized mug, filled it, topped it up with milk and took it to the breakfast counter, where he was already set up with the laptop.

The rising sun shrouded the entire room in gold and instead of feeling his lack of sleep, he felt energised. A real buzz in his veins.

Yes, he was worried. About Hannah. Their friendship. And, of course, their unborn child.

He'd spent half the night researching complications, the other half looking at the best healthcare in the area. He'd shortlisted some clinics and was ready to present it all to her.

He'd meant what he'd said—she wasn't alone, they were going to get through this together.

He recalled her soft-spoken question as she'd drifted off to sleep, a question he wasn't even sure she was aware she'd voiced, and it teased at the protected confines of his heart.

'What did I do to deserve a friend like you?'

He'd responded simply and quietly. *'You were you.'*

Though friend-turned-lover-turned-friend-again

was a dizzying adjustment, and one he needed to get a handle on because he couldn't forget what this was…

Friendship.

No more. No less.

She could never give him her heart, and he could never be with someone who gave him anything less. A child, on the other hand…his own flesh and blood…the strangest fluttering kicked off in his gut. Feeding the buzz.

'Morning.'

He jumped to his feet, his coffee spilling down his fresh white T and searing his skin. He flapped it away with a curse, doing a rapid dance as his eyes lifted to find her in the master bedroom doorway.

'Oh, God, I'm sorry!' she blurted, guilt turning her cheeks pink as she hurried towards him and he stilled. Enraptured. Voice stolen by her and everything she was about. Her blonde hair tumbling around her shoulders, his T-shirt skimming her bare thighs. 'Is it burning? You need to get it off, quick!'

Her hands were on the hem of his T-shirt before he could even process a rational thought and suddenly she was the one frozen still, her eyes launching to his so close and she gasped, shot back. 'I'm sorry!'

'Hey, it's okay.' He choked out a laugh, the heat of the coffee nothing compared to the heat dousing his body head to toe. 'My fault for being so engrossed with the laptop.'

Though nothing could engross him more than her right now. He'd seen her in his clothes before—the odd dinner jacket at a work function when the chill had set in, a hoodie he'd lent her after she and Leon had stayed over for a late-night study session. But seeing her in the soft cotton, the deep blue bringing out the clear grey of her gaze, the golden hue to her hair enhanced by the rising sun, the colour in her cheeks…all against the backdrop of his home, the scene so cosy and so close to perfect.

'I've got it,' he said, filling the awkward silence as he finished what she'd started and tugged his shirt over his head, balling it up in his fist. 'I'll get rid of this and then I can sort you some breakfast, what do…you…?'

His question trailed away as he took in her hungry gaze that resided well below neck level… It wasn't food she was hungry for and the realisation had him all but offering himself to her. 'Hannah?'

Her eyes snapped to his and she was stuttering out, 'I'm—I'm not sure I can stomach anything… not just yet.'

She backed up a step, one hand fluttering to the back of her neck, the other gesturing around aimlessly as she averted her gaze. 'I'm sorry about the coffee.'

His lips twitched—did she know how adorable she was right now? Hannah and adorable were not two words that ever went together…but right now…

And then he remembered the symptoms she had listed and wanted to slap his libido-infused self. 'Are you feeling sick? Of course, you are. I'm sorry. Sit down. Please.'

He hurried around her, pulling out a chair, encouraging her into it. 'What can I get you?'

'A miracle cure?'

'I wish I could.'

'I'll settle for a coffee though.'

'Of course.'

'And maybe you should put a top on…'

Her cheeks burned as she said it, her eyes still hovering where she didn't want them to, and if he'd not been so keen on making her feel better he might have asked what the problem was, provoked the flame…

Instead he headed for the machine as she piped up, 'Maybe the T-shirt first?'

He changed direction. 'As you wish.'

'And you need to stop saying that.'

He paused on his way out. 'Saying what?'

She waved a hand at him. 'The as you wish thing.'

'And that's a problem because…?'

'It has a whole *The Princess Bride* thing about it, and I—'

'It has a what?'

'*The Princess Bride.* You know… Westley and Princess Buttercup?' She slapped a hand on the breakfast bar, turned on the stool to eye him. 'You do know what I'm talking about?'

He racked his brain and drew a blank. 'No, can't say I do.'

'It's a film…well, like most things it was a book first.'

'And "as you wish" is a line from it…?'

'Yes.' She looked away, no more info forthcoming as she toyed with the hem of his shirt that had risen higher in her seated position. Her exposed thighs—all soft and creamy—making him remember, making him fantasise.

And swallow.

And breathe.

'I still don't see why it's a problem…'

She didn't respond straight away. In fact, he wondered if she was going to at all and was about to move on and leave the question hanging in all its awkward glory when she said, ever so quietly, 'Because when Westley says it to Buttercup, what he really means is *I love you*…'

'Oh.'

Ohh…

He forced himself to breathe past the sudden friction in his throat, his chest…

Walked right into that one, you idiot.

'I'll just…' He gestured back towards his room and moved before he could dig himself an even deeper hole.

When he returned, she was sitting where he'd

left her, still twisting the hem of his shirt in a rare show of insecurity, and his heart quickened, his movements too as he tore his gaze away and headed for the coffee machine.

'My clothes look good on you.' He was trying to be conversational, yet it came out flirtatious and he pulled a face at the machine, grateful she couldn't see.

'Thank you for letting me borrow it…and thank you for letting me stay.'

'As I recall, I didn't really get much say in the matter. You were out for the count.'

She grimaced. 'I know. I think all the sleepless nights have finally caught up with me.'

He grabbed her a large mug and filled it before his brain and his research caught up with him. 'Actually, maybe caffeine isn't such a great idea.'

Her head shot up. 'Really?'

'It can increase your blood pressure and your heart rate, and neither are good for the baby.'

She stared back at him. 'If you think I'm going without my morning coffee you can think again… it's *one* coffee, Brendan, and it's all I've been having since I found out, so hand it over before I climb you like a tree and get it myself.'

His mouth quirked to one side. 'Now *that* I'd like to see.'

'Brendan! If you don't want to witness an angry pregnant lady, whose blood pressure is certainly through the roof, I suggest you hand me that mug. Now.'

He chuckled, his eyes caught in the fire of hers. 'It's all yours, baby.'

It was out before he could stop it and her lashes fluttered, her breath a sharp inhalation. Her hand dropped back slightly and then she was all grace and poise as she straightened and took it from him.

'I don't suppose now is the time to ask how you got me out of my clothes?'

He was part way to sipping his own coffee and stopped. Grateful it hadn't passed his lips as he recalled that sequence of events. 'You were wearing a vest so I figured lose the sweater, didn't want you to overheat, and the bottoms I did with my eyes closed. Scout's honour.'

She surprised him with a laugh. 'Scout's honour?'

'Yes, ma'am.'

She shook her head. 'I guess it's nothing you haven't seen before.'

Of all the things she had to say, she had to say the one thing that would paint her naked and in his bed. He turned away before the effect of that image formed behind his loose-fitting pants and had her seeing far too much.

Topping up his coffee, he took a much-needed break—from her, the provocative images and his own dizzying thoughts.

'What's this?'

'Huh?' He turned to see her sliding his notepad towards her and he shot across the distance, closing it with the pen still in the page.

Her eyes narrowed. 'Got a secret you don't want to share?'

'No, of course not.'

'Or is it a case of client confidentiality? And I thought I was a rare breed getting up before sunrise on a Saturday to work on a case…obviously not today.'

She cupped her mug in both hands, took a sip. The vision of morning bliss capturing his heart and his mind—if only this was how it could be, each and every day. Waking in the same home, sipping coffee together, working together… co-parenting together.

'Brendan?' She was staring at him, expectant, the notepad burning into his fingertips.

He should agree, say something along the lines of great minds, and leave it at that. *Should* but he couldn't. He'd never lied to Hannah. He'd omitted to tell her his true feelings but never actually lied.

'No, it's not work-related.' He slid the notebook back towards her. 'I was going to show you anyway, I just figured you might want a gentler start to the morning.'

'Oh…' She frowned, cautiously swapping the mug for the book. She scanned a page and the next, her grip tightening around the edge as she navigated back, taking in his scrawl.

'You've been busy.'

Her voice was devoid of emotion. Her eyes didn't leave the page.

'I couldn't sleep.'

'Clearly.'

'I want you to be okay, Han, you and the baby. There's so much we need to think about, but I think the first thing we—'

'Stop, Brendan.' She snapped the book closed, dropped it on the side and pressed her fingers to her cheeks that lacked the colour of moments before. She looked pale and grey and—

'Are you going to be sick? Do you need a bowl? A flannel? Some water?'

'I just need you to stop.'

He paused halfway to opening a cupboard and turned back to her. 'Stop?'

'Yes!'

'I'm trying to help.'

'And it's too much. I'm not some case you need to evaluate and plan out.'

He frowned. 'Of course, you're not, but don't you think it's better to get up to speed sooner rather than later?'

'And I'm not even two months pregnant yet, as you so rightly informed me, anything can happen.'

He rounded the breakfast bar and took her hands in his. 'And I'm sorry I said those things, I didn't want to scare you. But don't you see, by getting to grips with it all now we stand a much better chance of having this baby, healthy and happy.'

She stared up at him, eyes wide, lips parted. Stunned was one word to describe her look. Terrified was another. She pulled away from him, took up her mug. 'And right now, I want to take it one day at a time.'

'Of course. That's why I've been through and researched the best antenatal clinics in the area. I've ranked them according to location, accessibility, facilities, ratings—the cost is inconsequential. I'll cover everything you need.'

'I can make my own medical appointments,' she said quietly. 'And pay for them too.'

'I know, but—'

'I mean it, Brendan. We do this my way or—or—'

'Or what?' He went cold. 'The highway?' His laugh was harsh. 'You're going to cut me out like you did two years ago.'

Her eyes shot to his. 'I never cut you out. *You* walked away from me.'

'Because you didn't give me a choice.'

'No. I just didn't give you the response you wanted. Are you going to do the same now?'

'No.' Brendan crossed his arms, tension pulling his entire frame taut, his eyes dark with recalled memories and the present battle. 'I'll never turn my back on the mother of my child.'

He said it with extra care, as though he knew

she was freaking out and was so close to grabbing her clothes—wherever they were—and fleeing.

'Whether you like it or not, appreciate it or not, Hannah, you've become the most important person in the world to me and I will do everything in my power to be there for you and my child when they are born.'

He was being too good. Too nice.

Teasing her with so much care and attention.

The kind she'd never known from anyone. Not even her mother had fussed over her in this way. She'd been the mum. She'd been the parent. Taking care of her and Jessie, having no one to turn to but herself. And it was far safer to keep it that way.

The one good thing to come out of her marriage was the reinforcement of that belief.

But Brendan was trying to shatter it. He was making it too easy to change, too easy to lean on him, to depend on him…last night had proven that. She'd let him comfort her and fallen asleep in his arms—safe, content, protected. And it would be so easy to get addicted to that feeling.

Addicted to something she had no control over, something that could quite easily be taken away too, and therein lay the root cause of her fear.

Control.

She'd lost it when Leon had asked for a divorce, shattering a life she had spent over a decade building. Lost it all the more when she'd caved to her feelings and fallen into bed with Brendan.

And her unexpected pregnancy was the result. But she wouldn't see it as a punishment.

She covered her stomach with her palm, assuring the innocent little bean—because he or she was the size of a bean, she'd seen that in Brendan's thorough notes—that it didn't matter that they weren't planned, they would be loved and cherished, protected and nurtured. They would never question their own worth. Ever.

Though the doubt remained… Could she do the loving, the cherishing, the nurturing? She could protect them with her all, but that emotional bond…?

'At least you didn't say "if"…' she said quietly, her voice cracking with it all.

'At least I didn't say…' He frowned and then his eyes widened with realisation, one hand reaching out to cover hers. 'I'm sorry, Han. It just feels very fragile right now, something as unexpected as this, something as huge and profound, it's hard not to become attached and I guess I'm doing everything I can to manage that feeling.'

This she understood, this struck a chord and then some.

'But I tell you what,' he said. 'I'll make a deal with you. I'll quit being the pessimist if you promise to listen to the experts and do what's best for you and the baby.'

He held out his hand for her to shake and she eyed it, preparing herself for the renewed contact and failing to steel herself against the warming current that pulsed through her, making her ache, making her want…

She crossed her legs. 'Deal.'

'And you'll book the appointment first thing Monday?'

'Yes.' He was still holding her hand and she didn't want to let him go…which was enough for her to force herself to do so. She turned on her stool and dragged the notebook towards her. His list, as pessimistic as it was, was far safer than what he was doing to her inside. She blamed it on the recent sight of him half naked but had a feeling he could be dressed in a binbag and she'd still be doing the drooling, the aching, the wanting.

'I'm really going to miss my mid-morning fix,' she said, focusing on his list of things to be avoided and praying he didn't notice the sudden pitch to her voice.

'Back to the coffee already?'

'It's everything.'

'You can still have decaf.'

She shuddered. 'And what would be the point in that?'

'Spoken like a true addict.'

'Guilty as charged. It's my one true vice. I can leave the alcohol, the chocolate…' But could she leave the sex with Brendan?

Where was her mind at? Was this a symptom of pregnancy too? Raging hormones that had her hanging on his every touch, fantasising about it, craving it?

'At least you can get the placebo hit with decaf.'

Was there an equivalent for sex?

A laugh blurted out of her.

'Don't knock it until you try it. I'll brew you one up.'

Thank heaven he didn't know the true cause of her fluster. 'You have decaf in?'

'Don't most people?'

'I'm not most.'

He shook his head, walked away... 'No, you're really not.'

'What was that?'

'Nothing, Han, nothing at all.'

Her knees started to bob as she gripped the stool beneath her, eyes taking in his rear and noticing things she hadn't seen before. The hint of curl in his hair when it was stripped of product, the broadness of his shoulders, the muscles that flexed beneath the fabric of his T. How narrow his waist was and how pert his...

Stop!

But she couldn't. She'd never seen Brendan stripped of his designer suits, high-end jeans, sweaters, shirts, the early-morning sun casting him in gold and giving the entire kitchen a cosy, homely feel.

Only it wasn't her home, their home; it was his.

But she could almost believe it was theirs...

And in loungewear, he was bordering on normal, a very appealing, 'want to wrap my arms around you and kiss you until the sun is high in the sky' normal. Because that was what normal couples, normal families did, right? It was what she'd witnessed as a child on the rare occasion she'd risked staying at a friend's house. Witnessed it. Envied it. And got over it.

Because it wasn't for her.

And that was okay.

But now...

Was this the mythical biological clock ticking? Sprung to life by the surprising turn her life had taken.

It felt more like a ticking time bomb—the countdown having started the second she'd awoken in his bed enshrouded in his scent, accelerated with his naked chest and become so much more with every caring word that had left his lips. She pressed a fist to her own as the morning sickness rose with the panicked beat of her heart.

She needed to bail.

'Do you think you could stomach some toast, or...?'

'I should go.' She was already standing when Brendan turned to face her and she focused on steadying her stool as it teetered, about to hit the deck. 'Where are my things?'

He frowned. 'You really should have something to eat first...'

'I'm good.' She ignored the way her heart beat harder as he stepped closer and she backed up. 'My things?'

'If you mean your clothes, they're being laundered. They should be back within the hour.'

'You sent my clothes to be *cleaned*?' And there he went again being all kind and thoughtful…

'It's a perk of the building.'

'But I…' She bobbed from one foot to the other, suddenly aware of how short his shirt was when his eyes dipped to her exposed thighs and her skin burned, her body throbbed… She tugged the fabric lower as if it would somehow help and sidestepped towards the master. 'I'll grab a shower, then.'

'Hang on…'

She was almost to the door and she paused, expectant and nervous—would he ask her to stay? And if he did, what should she say?

You really have to ask yourself that…?

'Don't you want to take your coffee with you if it is to be your precious one?'

She blushed, a frustrating sense of disappointment attacking her unbidden. She shouldn't be disappointed. She should be happy he was letting her leave without a fight.

Though the appeal of her apartment, her apartment that she had once shared with Leon, was non-existent. It was safe though. Safe from this.

She stepped forward, lowering her gaze so he couldn't see her thoughts—he seemed to read her like an open book and that wasn't a thought she wanted to make him privy to. She took the coffee from him with a hushed, 'Thank you.'

'And maybe dinner tonight? We should talk about how we're going to handle things at work. I'll need to be involved to some extent, and then there's Leon to consider. At some point we'll have to tell him.'

The foolish tickle of delight that he would want to see her again so soon was quickly doused by the mention of work and stampeded over by Leon.

Okay, now she was definitely going to be sick.

She covered her mouth, gave a panicked nod and fled. When she emerged from the bathroom half an hour later, a towel wrapped around her, there was a slice of wholemeal toast and a glass of milk on the bedside table. Her freshly laundered clothes were neatly laid out on the bed.

Tears pricked the backs of her eyes. Bloody Brendan. Adorable Brendan. Brendan and this baby, what were they doing to her?

'They recommend eating little and often to keep the nausea at bay.' His gentle voice came from the doorway, making her start. 'And I'm afraid caffeine might not be your friend when it comes to the morning sickness either. The milk is good though.'

'Been doing some more reading?' She didn't turn. She didn't want him to see her so weak. He'd already witnessed it enough.

'Apparently an empty stomach is hypersensitive to saliva so lining it with something like milk or yoghurt is a good idea and it can help neutralise the acid too.'

'Okay, Mr Pregnancy Expert.' She was proud that her voice didn't give away the emotion brimming beneath the surface. 'Now if you can leave me to get dressed, that would be great.'

And then she winced, her rudeness unacceptable. Just because she was so ill at ease, it didn't mean it was okay to take it out on him.

'Brendan!' She turned and he was gone. Her shoulders slumped and she bit her lip to bite back the tears.

'Yes?' He reappeared and her heart skipped a beat, her watery smile impulsive and bright.

'Thank you.' She waved a hand in the direction of the bed and the breakfast.

'It's the least I can do.'

And then he was gone and she just stood there, staring at the empty doorway, wondering how her life had got to this point. Thirty-eight and, for the first time in all her adult years, it was nothing like she'd planned it. She was unsure, unstable, an emotional wreck.

But she had Brendan—kind, thoughtful Brendan—and he had her back.

After everything, he still had her back.

So why are you still running from him?

* * *

'Hey, love...meet Brendan.'

Leon wrapped a possessive arm around her waist.

'Brendan, meet my better half.'

Hannah winced. She wasn't sure which bit was worse, the 'love' or the 'better half', but either way she hid it in a smile and offered her hand.

The tall, dark stranger she had seen standing beside Leon in the lecture theatre was even more striking up close. His rich brown eyes, both warm and sharp as they searched her own.

'It's a pleasure to meet you.'

His accent was refined, his voice smooth and deep, and his smile, those eyes...

'Though I think the name is Hannah and not "love".'

She pursed her lips, felt her heart dance, and then he took her hand in his and she forgot how to breathe...

Brendan Hart was like no man she'd ever met. Of that she was certain. And she took a moment to appreciate the chaos he'd stirred up within her before sweeping it all up into a box and clamping the lid down tight.

Safe. Controlled. Never to be examined again.

CHAPTER SEVEN

'YOU REALLY DIDN'T need to come.'

Hannah said it to the passing world outside, her body angled away from him as he drove.

'I wanted to.'

'It was hardly a revelatory meeting.'

'I don't know, it was a first for me.'

'Funny.' It wasn't judging by her tone.

'And I think it was useful for me to be there. At least you don't have to relay all those questions on my family's medical history now.'

'I guess.'

He sighed. It was one thing being told it wasn't necessary for him to come, another to be told by her tone that she didn't want him there. He also hadn't seen her properly since she'd left his apartment Saturday morning and it was now Wednesday, an eternity in his overly concerned book.

'Why is it such a problem that I came?'

'Because you should be working, not ferrying me around.'

'This was more important.'

She clenched her fists upon her lap and he felt the gesture to his core.

'You need to get used to it, Hannah, I'm not—'

The car chimed with an incoming call and he checked the display: Natasha Austin.

'You should get it,' Hannah said, seeing who it was.

'Should I, now? Not trying to avoid the conversation, are we?'

She gave a small shrug and looked away. 'Could be important.'

Brendan shook his head and bit back the retort, *Not as important as you*, sensing it would only make matters worse.

He answered the call. 'Morning, Natasha.'

'Morning, love, I hope I haven't caught you at a bad time.'

'No, you're fine, I'm driving to the office.'

'Handsfree?'

'Of course.'

'Well, I won't keep you, it's just…'

The phone went quiet and he checked the display—still connected. 'Natasha?'

'It's Joel.'

When is it not?

He glanced at Hannah, could virtually see her ears pricking. 'What about him?'

'I spoke to him the other day and though he said he'd get back to Simone about her engagement party, he still hasn't and it's only a few weeks away and though it's not going to be an issue if he turns up last minute, it would just be nice to…'

'To have an RSVP?'

She sighed. 'Yes. I can't help feeling that the reason he hasn't replied is that he doesn't want to go back on his word. At least if he says he'll be there, we can trust him to turn up. Don't you think?'

'Perhaps.'

'Can you speak to him, Brendan? Please? He's more likely to listen to you.'

'I can try but you know Joel, he's a law unto himself.' It was out before he could stop it and inside, he winced, praying Hannah didn't read too much into it. He shouldn't have answered the call. He should have known Natasha would want to talk about Joel and, next to Leon, he was the last man Hannah needed to hear about with Jessie still being stuck on an island with him.

'I know, love, I know. But it's been two years since Katie passed, God rest her soul, and I'm scared if he doesn't come back soon, he never will.'

Her voice cracked and Brendan's fists flexed around the steering wheel. 'He'll come back, Natasha, don't doubt it.'

'I hope you're right, love.'

'I'll make it right.' He said it under his breath, too quiet for Natasha to hear but Hannah did. Her eyes flitted to him, but he kept his own fixed on the road. 'I'll call him and get him to speak to Simone.'

'And RSVP?'

He nodded. 'And RSVP.'

'You'll make sure he comes, won't you?'

'I'll do everything I can.'

Silence and then, 'Thank you, Brendan.' Her voice wavered. 'That boy is so lucky to have you.'

His lips twitched at the boy reference—they were thirty-five but in Natasha's eyes they would be teenagers for ever.

'And I him.' Because he was, Joel had pulled him out of his own rut after the death of his parents, protected him from the bullies who'd had a field day with the court case, the rumours, the gossip. 'I'll speak to you soon, Natasha.'

'Take care, love.'

He cut the call and sensed Hannah's gaze still on him, could sense her burning questions and concern too. 'Look, I know it sounds bad, but you have to understand Joel's been through a lot and—'

'And now he's on an island with my sister, who has a penchant for stray animals.'

'You're likening Joel to a stray animal?'

'Stray, wounded, damaged—however you put it, it doesn't matter. My sister is a romanticist, she's going to do everything in her power to "fix" him.' She did air quotes around the word.

'I've been trying to fix him for two years and got nowhere. To be frank, I could do with all the help I can get.'

* * *

Hannah stared at him. The heartfelt desperation that had crept into his voice triggered an ache deep within her chest and for once, she stopped thinking of Jessie, stopped thinking of the baby that she was so scared of failing and thought of Brendan. The man behind the capable mask.

The man who had been tasked with the impossible—to bring the wandering man back home.

She wished she hadn't told him to take the call but then Natasha would have got hold of him eventually and applied the exact same pressure.

'It's not right that they put all this on you.'

He flicked her a look. 'What do you mean?'

'Asking you to make sure he gets to this engagement party, sends an RSVP, all of it... He's not your responsibility. He has two brothers that could be on at him too.'

'Been Googling him, have we?'

Her cheeks warmed. 'I felt it was important to understand all there was about the man stranded on an island with my sister.'

He pressed his lips together, scanned the street. 'I'd rather you asked me than scoured the Internet. You know the press aren't to be trusted.'

And he knew that better than most with his history, but she wasn't stupid, she'd fact-checked enough to get a good enough picture of the man her sister was now on vacation with.

And even if his playboy antics had been exag-

gerated, Joel's mental state was clearly question-
able. It was his sister's engagement party after all,
and Joel was the eldest. With his father gone, he
was the man of the family, a responsibility that
should see him taking an active role in the cele-
brations, not running from them. Just as Hannah
had stepped up in her own family, Joel should be
doing the same. How could she not question his
mental state?

And how could she trust Brendan to give her an
honest response when he wouldn't want to worry
her and he'd want to protect Joel too. But maybe
she should have given him that chance first.

'I'm sorry, I should have come to you. But how
do I know you're not going to paint him in a rosier
light just to stop me worrying?'

'Because I'm no liar, and you should know that
well enough. And just because Joel isn't my blood,
it doesn't mean he's not my brother in every other
way. He's a good man, Han.'

'So you keep saying, but he's also the man who
hasn't RSVP'd to his only sister's engagement
party and has his mother at her wits' end worrying about him. He's put you in a tricky position
and, to be frank, he's the last person Jessie needs
in her life right now.'

'As far as Jessie goes, I trust him to do right
by her.'

'And his sister? His family? Will he do right
by them?'

'Eventually. I just need to get through to him.'

'And what if you can't?'

'Then at least I will have tried.'

She nodded, but she could see that failure wasn't an option in his book.

She reached out, unthinking, her hand soft on the solid heat of his thigh. She swallowed. Why were suit trousers so thin…or was he just super-hot?

And, oh, God, there went her cheeks again.

'You'll do your best. I know you will.' She focused on her intent to reassure him and not the heat her own actions had sparked. 'But he's a grown man, Brendan, you can't control him. He has to do this for himself and you can't blame yourself for the path he chooses to take.'

He turned to her, the look in his eye unreadable. 'Sounds similar to something I told you recently…'

'You mean Jessie?'

'Yes, I mean Jessie. It's time you let her be the grown-up she is and quit monitoring her every move.'

'I don't—'

His eyes were back on her, sharp and astute.

'Okay. I will. Just as soon as she's clear of your Joel.'

He shook his head, looked back to the road, braking as the traffic lights ahead turned red.

The muscle beneath her fingers flexed and she snatched her hand back, clutched it in her lap.

It was no use though, her palm still tingled from the contact, the throbbing ache, warm and needy and low in her abdomen, reminding her of everything she still craved from him and couldn't let herself have. Not without muddying the waters and risking their friendship further.

Muddying your way of living and risking your heart, you mean.

She nipped her lip until she thought she might draw blood and only then did she release her hand and take up her phone.

She'd message Jessie, a quick check-in to make sure Joel was keeping his distance. Distract herself with her sister's life rather than the mess in her own. But as it happened, Jessie had already messaged her.

'You have to be kidding me!'

'What?'

She spun to face him. 'Did you know Joel is staying on at the villa? That's he's staying right up until the time she *leaves*.'

He grimaced, cursed under his breath. 'Anton may have mentioned something, but I didn't think it was definite.'

'And you didn't think to tell me?'

'I wanted to check in with Joel first, find out for sure.'

'You should have told me.'

'I didn't want to worry you any more than you already are. The midwife warned you that your blood pressure is higher than they'd like, you're malnourished, and your—'

She cursed. 'I knew I shouldn't have let you come.'

'And I'm glad I came, so get over it.'

'Get over it?'

'Yes! Jessie will be fine! You have a baby to worry about now, plough your energy into them and let your sister live her life.'

But she wasn't listening to him, she was already dialling her sister's number. Not that Jessie was picking up. She sent her a message demanding she called her back as soon as possible and sank back into her chair, frowning as she registered the unfamiliar route Brendan was taking through London. 'This isn't the way to the office...'

'We're picking up the pregnancy supplements the midwife recommended on the way.'

'I'm quite capable of doing that myself.'

'When exactly? You're already two months pregnant and the midwife made it clear you should have been taking folic acid long before now.'

'Will you stop lecturing me?' He was poking at her insecurities, pricking at her fear that she would make an awful mother... 'I can't bear it.'

'I'm not lecturing you.' He stared back at her. 'I'm looking after you both, though if you want my opinion...'

She opened her mouth to tell him she didn't, but he wasn't waiting on her.

'…maybe it does you good to feel how your sister must feel under your watchful eye, your constant questioning and suffocating attention.'

'You don't know what you're talking about.'

'I've known you for fifteen years. I have a pretty good idea.'

He wasn't wrong, was he?

Hadn't she all but admitted she lived her life for her sister? Woke up worrying about her, went to sleep worrying about her. Hadn't she been in constant touch with her since her arrival in Mustique, failing to give her any true freedom?

'But I do it out of love.'

Something flickered over his expression, his mouth parting to say something as a horn honked behind. The lights had turned green and whatever he'd been about to say left his face. He looked back to the road, put the car into gear and moved off.

Fear stopped her asking him what it was, fear contending with the part of her that she was desperately trying to ignore.

She didn't want to know. She didn't need to know.

Her heart though…her neglected and very much ignored heart cried out to hear it.

Maybe she wasn't so different from her mother after all.

* * *

'Mum, I got an extra tenner at the café!'

She kicked the back door closed behind her and slid the takeaway boxes onto the kitchen table.

'You know what that means! It's takeaway pizza for tea!'

Her mum entered the room, her perfume reaching her first. 'Oh, Hannah, darling. I'm so glad you're home.'

She frowned at her mum's dress, the full face of make-up, the twinkling eyes, and felt the dread set in. 'Where are you going?'

'Dominic has invited me out for dinner.' She was too busy fastening one earring to notice her daughter's face. 'Isn't that wonderful?'

'Dominic? As in the guy who was supposed to take you out last week, and the week before, but bailed last minute?'

She wafted a hand at her. 'He had good reason.'

'Which was…?'

'I don't know, I can't remember. Don't look at me so, Han. Don't you want your mother to find happiness again?'

It was the same every time her mother met a man who showed her more than an ounce of attention. She and Jessie were forgotten.

'What about our Friday girls' night?' She lifted the boxes that now felt limp in her hands. 'I bought pizza.'

'All the more for you and Jessie to enjoy, love.

And I will pay you back for it. Just as soon as Dominic gives me the tips from the pub. Now, be good, won't you? Give Jessie a kiss for me and don't wait up.'

She watched her mother skip out the door, knowing that she wouldn't see that money. Knowing even more that she would wait up. Because the last time her mother had left them to go on a date she'd only just managed to save Jessie from witnessing their mother curled up on the sofa the next morning, still clothed, make-up streaked down her cheeks, an empty wine glass in her hand and with another broken heart.

And no child needed to see their mother like that. Not ever.

CHAPTER EIGHT

'THAT'S HARDLY FAIR.'

Brendan looked up at the sound of Hannah's voice, the desperation in her tone putting him on high alert. He'd been talking to Hannah's PA about her schedule, surreptitiously getting a feel for Hannah's workload while he killed time waiting for her to arrive.

Killed time and tried to ignore the mounting worry that she wasn't in yet. Eight a.m. was late by her standards but here she was—black skirt suit, high heels, hair smoothed back in a ponytail—and striding across the office with her phone to her ear. She faltered as soon as she saw him, her eyes widening, the clip of her heels on the glossy floor slowing.

Was she going to bail?

He straightened, primed to go after her but then she lowered the phone and her trusty mask slid into place. Anyone within earshot would think they'd imagined the hint of desperation as she'd spoken down the phone...he didn't.

She continued towards him, her make-up concealing any pallor but the creases either side of her eyes hadn't eased, her smile was tight and the hand holding her phone wasn't quite steady.

'What's wr—?'

'Not here.' She cut him off, her eyes falling to her PA. 'Jackie, can you hold my calls for an hour, please?'

'Morning to you too, boss.'

She softened a little, her smile turning apologetic. 'Sorry, I've not had my caffeine fix this morning.'

'You need me to pop to Joe's, grab you one?'

'No need.' Her eyes drifted to him. 'I think I'm going to give some herbal infusions a go.'

As much as he loathed the sickness plaguing her, he'd like to think her edginess stemmed from it. But he suspected it had more to do with whoever had been on the other end of the phone… Leon? Jessie? A case?

Then she looked to him. 'Are you waiting to—?'

'Hey, Hart, good to hear the news!' Jonathan, a senior associate with the ability to magic himself out of the woodwork, grinned at him as he passed by, cutting Hannah off. 'America's loss is the UK's gain, that's what I say.'

Surprised that news of his transfer had already broken, he barely had time to register him with a nod. Then he saw Hannah's face and realised it hadn't broken, Jonathan had just managed to get the lowdown somehow. Considering the man was a known sycophant, constantly schmoozing up to the managing partners, he didn't have to ponder too hard.

She strode into her office and he followed her in, closing the door behind him.

'What was that about?' She dropped her bag onto the desk and removed her long woollen coat, which seemed overkill for this time of year. Even for him and he was accustomed to New York, which was a few degrees higher than London. Was she feeling the cold? Was it the weight loss?

She placed her coat on the rack and returned to her desk, looked at him over the top. 'Brendan?'

Parking his concern, he answered her. 'I've requested a transfer.'

'From New York to here?'

He nodded, sensing her raised hackles and refusing to rise with them.

'And I'm the last to know about it?'

'No, it wasn't supposed to be announced until month end. I'd only talked it over with the managing partners yesterday and intended to tell you today.'

'And yet, Jonathan knows all about it.'

He pocketed his hands. 'Jonathan knows everything about everyone in this building, you know that.'

She didn't correct him.

'Ted wouldn't stand for that kind of behaviour stateside.'

'Yes, well, Ted isn't here. You have Andrew to

deal with this side of the pond…then again, that shouldn't be a problem considering you two go way back.'

'Jealous?' He fired back at her, a smile teasing at his lips, and she huffed, a captivating spark of fire returning to her eyes. He loved Hannah like this. Feisty, quick-witted, sexy as…

'Like I need to be.'

He ran his teeth over his bottom lip, their old competitive camaraderie arching between them and, for the briefest spell, the reality of their situation was forgotten. They were simply Hannah and Brendan—firm friends, colleagues, first-class lawyers.

And then she blinked and lowered her gaze, her voice sombre as she asked, 'So why exactly are you doing this?'

His brows drew together. 'Isn't it obvious?'

Gingerly, she lowered herself to her seat, her black skirt suit doing her skin no favours. He'd been wrong about the make-up. The pink in her cheeks must have been *au naturel* as she'd crossed the office because it was noticeably absent now.

'You don't need to transfer location for me.'

He clenched his jaw, took up the seat opposite her. Why couldn't she be like the many women he'd dated over the years—all wanting more? More of his time. More of his commitment. Just more.

Not Hannah though, she'd never need anyone…

And now you sound like Leon.

And he knew it wasn't true.

'I'm doing it for you *and* our child.'

Her eyes widened, flitting to the open office beyond the glass.

'They can't hear us.'

She shifted in her seat. 'I'd rather not talk about it here.'

'Then don't ask me about my motivations.'

'You should have told me first.'

'I didn't know it was possible until yesterday and, let's face it, other than the appointment on Wednesday you've been avoiding me all week, so how was I supposed to tell you?'

'An email would have sufficed.'

'An email, right.' He nodded. 'Is that how you want to play this?'

'This?'

'Our interaction—no face to face contact unless strictly necessary…?'

She took an unsteady breath and he got the distinct impression she was forcing herself to maintain eye contact. Did she really want him gone that badly? Or was it something else? Was he getting to her in the same way she got to him? Did she want to shove the desk aside and plant a kiss right on—?

'I haven't been avoiding you. I've been busy and email is—' she wet the lips he was suddenly fixated on '—convenient.'

'Right.' He took in the colour returning to her cheeks, the way she crossed and uncrossed her legs. 'Convenient.'

She *was* feeling it and it should have made him feel better…instead it only served to heighten his own frustration. He'd missed her. That was what it came down to. Not even forty-eight hours apart and he'd felt her absence. It was foolish but no less true.

He drummed his fingers against the edge of the arm rest, used the rhythmic contact to soothe his pulse.

'How long are you going to be working here for?'

'Indefinitely.'

Her eyes flared. 'You don't need to do this. Uproot your life in New York because of this.'

'Don't I?'

'People have—' her eyes flitted to the office beyond the glass as she leaned forward slightly and lowered her voice '—babies together all the time and don't necessarily live on the same continent.'

His eyes narrowed and he raised his hand to his chin, ran his finger under his lower lip as he considered her. What was she really upset about?

'Do you honestly think I would be happy going back to New York knowing you are carrying my child, knowing you are carrying my child and feel like you do?'

'I'm not going to terminate the pregnancy, Brendan!'

His jaw pulsed. 'That wasn't what I meant.'

'Then what did you mean? Do you not trust me to do what's right by our baby? To put their health first?'

'No, Han. Nothing like that.'

'Then what?'

'I was talking about *your* health. The sickness. Your weight. I was talking about the fact that you're wearing a coat for the depths of winter when it's only spring.'

She sank back, her eyes flickering.

'I'm talking about wanting to be here to look after you both, to help as and when you need it.'

'I'm perfectly capable of looking after us, Brendan.' Her hand fell to her stomach and he wondered if she was even conscious of it.

'I know, but, as I made it very clear to you, I'm not going anywhere. I'm here to take care of you and our baby.'

'Like you took care of the whole Jessie and Joel situation?'

He did a double take, surprised by the rapid change in focus. But then, this was Hannah and Jessie was her constant worry. 'Can we stick to one topic at a time?'

'That was Jessie on the phone.'

Obviously not...

'But it must be what, three in the morning out

there?' His gut rolled. 'What's happened? Did she call you?'

'No. I called her.'

That was a relief. 'Did you forget the time difference?'

'No. She's been ignoring my calls.'

Not a relief, then. 'She's on holiday, surely the fact that her phone isn't glued to her should be seen as a good thing.'

'It would be if it wasn't for a certain house guest.'

'Joel assures me he's keeping his distance.'

'Really?' Her brows rocketed, her laugh pitched. 'Well, according to my sister, he's the best thing that's ever happened to her so if that's what you call keeping his distance, I'd love to see what he managed up close and personal.'

He cursed. 'He promised me.'

'Did you get it in writing?' Her voice dripped with sarcasm.

'Hannah, please, they're adults, they'll be fine. You shouldn't let this stress you out, think of your blood—'

'Bring up my blood pressure again and I'll be seeing Ted myself to put an end to your transfer.'

If she'd struck him, it couldn't have hurt more. 'Is that really what you want?'

She stared back at him, eyes unblinking, glossy pink lips pursed. And he was done being sweet.

'Do you honestly think you have that level of

power over me, over the managing partners? I'd love to know the reason you'll give.'

She shuddered, her lashes fluttering as though coming awake to herself and she reached across the desk, her palm soft on the wood. 'I'm sorry, Brendan, I shouldn't have said that.'

'No, you shouldn't have.'

'I'm just—'

She dragged in a breath, her eyes going to the window, and he caught the glistening edge to one. His chest tightened, his hand forming a fist beneath his chin as he fought the need to go to her. Pregnant women were hormonal, he told himself. Hannah wasn't your average woman, but she was still a woman. And she was still pregnant. She wasn't invincible.

And now that just sounded sexist and belittling and only made him feel worse.

'We fought.'

He almost didn't hear her. 'You and Jessie?'

She nodded. 'We don't ever fight.' She looked back to him. 'Not like that.'

'What about?'

'What do you think?'

'Specifically?'

'I warned her about Joel, said he wasn't to be trusted, not with his ongoing grief and his playboy reputation. She told me I didn't know what I was talking about, that she believed he was getting better, that she knew what she was doing. I, of course, told her she was wrong.'

'Maybe she's not wrong.'

'She's wrong, Brendan. He's pulled the wool over her eyes good and proper, and she's besotted. And he's going to break her heart. I just know it.'

'You don't know that at all.'

'I also landed you in it.'

He frowned. 'How so?'

'I told her about the engagement party, the fact he hadn't RSVP'd. I was using it as an example of his current state of mind but her takeaway was that you'd been bad-mouthing Joel behind his back and criticising him to me.'

'I see.' He was already in deep with one Rose sister, what was another? And Joel would understand…his friend knew it came from a good place. He wasn't worried about him in that moment, or Jessie for that matter, he was worried about the woman sitting before him.

'Sorry. I didn't mean to drag you into our fight, but I was desperate.'

'And don't you think you're projecting a little?'

'What do you mean?'

'I know Leon hurt you.'

She shook her head with a choked scoff. 'This has nothing to do with him.'

'No, then why have such a low opinion of Joel

if it isn't in some way fuelled by your own experience?'

'It has *nothing* to do with Leon.'

'But you don't even know Joel.'

'I know enough.'

Brendan nodded, his thoughts his own. And she wanted to know them, she wanted to know what had made his eyes glint and his frown deepen. 'Deflecting, then?'

'Deflecting?'

'All this focus on Jessie…is it because you don't want to think about what's happening between us?'

Us. There was no 'us'. And why did the mere suggestion that there was send her pulse racing and her mouth dry?

'Why can't I genuinely be worried for my sister?'

That's it, change the focus once more…

'Have you told her about Leon yet?'

'No.'

'What about the baby?'

'Don't be ridiculous, Brendan. If I haven't told her about Leon, I can hardly tell her that I'm pregnant. "Oh, hey little sis, you know my marriage that was so perfect, well, it's over. And you know Brendan, the kind and thoughtful friend who let you use his villa, well, we slept together and now I'm pregnant".'

The room fell silent in the wake of her bluntness, the magnitude of their situation weighing heavy in the air.

'It's hardly ideal, no, but I think it will do you good to talk to someone other than me about it. It's not good for you or the baby to keep bottling it up.'

'The phone is no place for that conversation.'

'It's better than nothing.'

'And like I told you, I'll tell her when she gets back… I only hope she's in a good enough state after Joel's finished with her to hear it.'

He was quiet for a moment, pensive with his thoughts. 'I'll call Joel.'

'I don't think it'll do any good.'

'Well, what do you want to do, fly out there and chaperone the pair of them?'

The thought hadn't even occurred to her. Not with her workload and the baby and the swirling ball of emotion that never seemed too far from the surface ever since they'd slept together. Not to mention the fact that she couldn't stop thinking of it. Of him. Replaying it over and over and wishing she could go back and change it. Or live in it for ever.

'Hannah?'

'Huh?'

'Are you seriously wanting to fly out there?'

'I hadn't considered it, but now you mention it…'

'You're serious?'

'It's an idea.'

'She's not even been there a fortnight. I thought you wanted to give her space.'

'And she's hardly had that with Joel hanging around.'

'Her holiday may not be panning out quite like you wanted, but there's nothing to say it's going badly. And though I can't control Joel, I can assure you that he's a good man, underneath all the press hype and his painful past. He's just trying to find his feet again after the loss of his wife.'

'But if he hurts her—'

He went very still. 'If he hurts her, then we're done.'

She gave a derisive laugh. 'He's your best friend, your brother for all intents and purposes, you can't seriously expect me to believe—'

'He promised me.'

There was a fierce burr to his tone that quit the incessant noise in her brain. Trust, that was what it came down to, and she trusted Brendan.

She also felt a whole lot more and it sent her head into a spin, the strange sense of sickness washing over her.

'Thank you.' She pressed herself up from the desk and forced a weak smile. 'I should get on and I'm sure you have work to be getting on with too.'

He was slower to stand and she couldn't ignore the concern in his gaze. 'Are you okay?'

'I will be.'

'Sickness?'

She gave the smallest of nods.

'Can I get you anything?'

'No.'

'Okay. Let me know if—'

'I will.'

He turned to leave and paused. 'Message Jessie and clear the air otherwise you'll only feel worse.'

She nodded, knowing he was right.

He walked away, his hand reaching for the door handle, and then a thought struck her.

'Wait.' Gingerly, she stepped out from behind her desk. 'What were you and Jackie discussing when I arrived?'

'Jackie?'

'My PA…'

'Nothing important.'

'Just small talk?'

'Not quite.' He turned to face her fully and there was something in his expression that had her on edge. 'I was checking over your schedule.'

Prickly heat spread across her skin. 'Why?'

'I wanted to see what I could assist with.' He held her eye, unperturbed by the storm he must sense was brewing. 'I'm going to be here for the foreseeable and I want to be sure you have the time to look after yourself and the baby.'

She closed the gap between them, so close his scent reached her—warm, masculine, so very inviting. Why did he have to smell so good? And what was it about his body heat that made her want to lean in and have him just hold her?

'I may be pregnant, Brendan, but I'm not incapable.' Her thoughts were at odds with her words, and she strengthened her tone. Unsure who she wanted to convince more, her or him. 'If you want to know my schedule you ask me, not my PA... and for the record, if I want help, I'll ask for it.'

'That's just it, Hannah, you don't ask.'

And then he left and the chill of the air con was nothing compared to the chill in her heart.

CHAPTER NINE

BRENDAN PAUSED ON the threshold of Hannah's apartment building and checked his phone again, making sure he hadn't misread it:

I'm sorry. Dinner at mine tomorrow night? Six p.m.?

It was simple, to the point, and confusing beyond measure. Not only was she apologising—for what he wasn't quite sure—she was inviting him to hers on a Saturday night when a week ago she'd insisted they meet at his to avoid tongues wagging.

Was this progress? Was she coming to terms with the future and this was a positive step forward?

He pressed the call button and waited...and waited...and finally, it connected. The door buzzing open. No verbal welcome, just the door... hardly encouraging.

He blew out a breath and stepped inside, opting for the stairs rather than the lift. Giving him time to...to what? Calm his nerves? Temper his expectations? Build up his barriers?

He was trying to stay guarded, to keep his feelings at bay, and failing at every turn. Doing right by her and the baby while also protecting himself from wanting what he knew she could never give was the hardest thing he'd ever had to do.

Knowing she was carrying his child—the very visceral reaction he had every time she touched a hand to her stomach, or their thoughts and conversation turned to that truth, he was undone by it.

'Brendan…'

He looked up and there she was. Standing in her open doorway, a tentative smile on her lips that he'd never seen her give before. Her clothes too were so unlike her. A baby-pink high-neck jumper, soft grey leggings, and thick fluffy socks. He was glad he'd opted for jeans and a sweater, rather than the shirt and trousers he'd been tempted to wear, because dinner with Hannah had always been a high-end affair. Even pizza night had seen her dolled to the nines.

'I hope you don't mind, what you see is what you get.' She lifted a hand to her hair that she'd tied in a somewhat messy knot atop her head. 'I fell asleep on the sofa and lost track of time.'

'Mind? You look—' her eyes flared and he checked himself '—adorable.'

Adorable was okay, right? It wasn't suggestive, flirtatious, contentious. Just true. And it wasn't the first time he'd thought it of her recently…it had been the same when she'd been wearing his shirt.

'Adorable?' Her cheeks warmed with her smile, her lack of make-up making the blush more evident and dialling up the adorable to the point of distraction. 'Come on in.'

He cleared his throat, wishing he could clear his wayward thoughts as easily, and entered the apartment, offering out the bottle in his hand. 'Apparently it's one of the best non-alcoholic sparkling varieties on the market, and I read that fizzy drinks can be easier to stomach.'

'You and your research...' But she was still smiling as she said it, the subtle roll of her eyes more playful than sarcastic. 'Thank you.'

'You're welcome.'

She led the way to the kitchen and he followed, dazed and ever more confused. First an apology, now this...

He scanned the apartment, noting how much it had changed since the last time he'd been here. Leon's modern art had gone—paintings the guy had never understood but invested in anyway. A future payoff, he'd said, claiming they looked the part when in reality they'd dominated the soft furnishing of the room, ruined the calm quality that had clearly been all Hannah. The cream sofa and the plush rugs, the warm wooden coffee table and sideboards with the scented candles and fresh ivory flowers.

The wedding pictures were notably absent, as was the huge flatscreen TV and sound system that had been more of an eyesore than a feature.

An array of monochrome photographs were artfully displayed instead, each capturing a certain theme or mood. Ballet dancers mid-movement, a woman in a window seat staring out, a family of wellies lined up in a doorway in order of size…

'Do you like them?'

He jumped, not realising she was so close.

'Sorry—' that tentative smile was back '—I didn't realise I'd lost you to them.'

'They're really eye-catching.'

'Thank you.'

He studied her face. There was something about the way she said it, the way she now looked at them. 'They're yours? You took them?'

She nodded, handing him a glass of the sparkling wine he had brought. 'Leon wasn't much for photography so I never thought to do anything with them. They're ancient but they still have that appeal…'

'I didn't realise you were something of a photographer.'

She gave a short laugh. 'Hardly, I haven't picked up a camera in years, haven't had the time.'

'Maybe it's time you made time…these really are amazing.'

'Adorable. Amazing.' Her eyes sparkled as she looked to him. 'You're really ramping it up with the compliments tonight.'

'I'm serious, Hannah, I can't believe you had this talent all along and you don't use it.'

'When do we have the time?'

'I mean it, you should make time.'

'Perhaps…'

He turned to face her head-on. 'When the baby comes you'll need to find time. Have you thought about how you'll balance everything then?'

'For a guy who not one week ago was concerned I wouldn't carry this baby full term, you really have changed your tune.'

'I told you, no more pessimism.'

'Well, I have been thinking about it. There are plenty of options. A live-in nanny, childminder, nursery…'

'I meant finding time for you, you and the baby, family time, not putting them in someone else's care.'

She wet her lips, her eyes searching his. 'They'll have the two of us for that. I don't think family time will be an issue.'

He wanted to say more, he wanted to tell her he didn't want a live-in nanny, he didn't want a childminder. Yes, he liked the benefit of social interaction at a nursery, but he wanted them as parents to be the primary caregivers. But she was already moving away, back towards the open-plan kitchen, and he sensed it wasn't up for debate, not this second anyway.

They were making progress…he could feel it. A step towards a better place, a better relationship and that could only provide the grounding for a better future.

'I've made lasagne, I hope that's okay.'

'You cooked?'

She laughed. 'Don't say it like that.'

'Need I remind you the last time you cooked, we all missed work the next day.'

She grimaced. 'I'm never going to live that down, am I? But I swear it was the prawns, not my culinary skills.'

'You keep telling yourself that.'

She reached out to shove his shoulder gently before moving away. 'Carry on like that and you can go hungry.'

He laughed and for the first time in a long while, he relaxed and enjoyed her company. Almost like old times, minus Leon's watchful gaze and the worry that the guy would read too much in something Brendan said or did, that he'd catch him watching Hannah a fraction longer than he should, or, worse, that he would just come right out and tease him as he had on his wedding day. Take his biggest secret and declare it to the one person who could never know.

'You going to just stand there or join me?' She was sitting down at the intimate little table, the lasagne steaming in the middle with a salad bowl and a sliced baguette either side. Her mouth was laughing but her eyes were curious. Wondering where his head had gone, he was sure, and he smiled back at her.

'Just weighing up whether I really want to be able to run tomorrow.'

She pursed her lips. 'I think I preferred it when you were laying on the compliments.'

'A man can't win.'

'When that man is you, absolutely not.' But she was teasing him still, her whole face was alive with it and as he joined her at the table he dipped to her ear.

'Forever the competitive one, Ice. You always did like a challenge.'

He took the seat opposite her and basked in her sudden glow. Knowing he'd put that warmth in her cheeks, that the chemistry still simmered beneath the surface…and he relished its presence.

Relished it a little too much.

'And you're saying you present that challenge.'

'If the shoe fits…'

Her eyes dipped over him, hot and hungry. Her delicate throat bobbed. Then, 'We should eat before this gets cold.'

His grin was uncontainable. 'I couldn't agree more.'

Though as much as he loved Italian, it was a certain British woman who had his tastebuds tingling…

Not that she'd want to know it.

Or maybe, in this moment, she would?

CHAPTER TEN

OH. MY. GOD.

What was wrong with her?

She was a simmering pot of lustful imaginings and squirming in her chair like a child unable to sit still. But the pulsing ache he'd kickstarted down low when he'd whispered beside her ear wouldn't quit and squeezing her thighs together was having zero effect. Except to make it worse.

Pregnancy had a lot to answer for and sheer, unadulterated lust was right up there at the top. She ought to Google it.

Or she could ask the oracle himself?

So, Brendan, in all your research did you happen to come across something that said pregnancy turns a woman into a rampant rabbit?

She laughed, choking on the mouthful of food she had just taken.

His eyes shot to hers, concern flashing in his sexy dark depths—*see, sexy!* Since when had she labelled his eyes as sexy? Any eyes, for that matter? Her sister would have a field day if she could hear her meandering mind now.

'Are you okay?'

'Absolutely!' She covered her mouth, swallowed her food with a nod. 'Just my mind wandering.'

'Care to share?'

A pitched laugh. 'No.'

He cocked his head to the side, a smile tugging at his lips.

'Is it okay?' She gestured to the food, aiming to distract him.

'It's great… You've scrubbed up on your cooking skills.'

'Not really. I can make lasagne with my eyes closed. The prawns were a bit of a Leon-inspired adventure.'

He chuckled, taking a slice of bread and using it to scoop up some sauce. 'Well, Leon should have kept quiet. This would have done perfectly.'

'It was one of Jessie's favourites when she was little.'

'Your mum's recipe?'

'Ha, no. My mother wasn't what you'd call domesticated.'

'So, you cooked?'

She could see the surprise in his face.

'I'll have you know that I'd mastered the art of the microwave by the age of eight and improved from there.'

'You fed yourself as a kid?'

She chewed over her food, washed it down with some water. 'Me and Jessie. She's ten years younger than me so by the time she was ready for real food I could sort a meal. It might not have been balanced but I made sure she ate. And Mum when she was home. To be honest, I didn't think anything of it at the time, but as I got older and visited friends' houses, I realised my life wasn't quite the norm.'

'That must have been tough.'

She shrugged. 'It was all I knew.'

His frown deepened. 'But where were your parents? I know you said your father wasn't the best but...'

'Fighting, drinking, socialising...'

The creases either side of his eyes deepened, the sadness in their depths too.

'Don't get me wrong, my mother loved us...my father not so much. The day he left the tension in the entire house lifted, but then Mum never did so well on her own so we had the constant cycle of heartbreak. She'd meet a man, fall instantly, then the next week she'd be heartbroken again. It took a long time for her to give up on love entirely and be happy on her own.'

'And you had to live through it all...'

'It wasn't all bad. We had some fun times. She was more of a friend than a mother.'

'But she turned you into the mother?'

She shrugged. 'We survived it, didn't we? I got a job as soon as I could, brought money in, made sure there was food in the cupboards and that Jessie got to school. Or at least, tried. She was a handful as a child, acting out, playing truant, she had awful nightmares and anxiety attacks that would see her trying to run away from anything that was forced upon her.'

'Did she grow out of it?'

'Eventually. But her teens weren't much better, she was forever getting in with the wrong crowd... the wrong men.'

Realisation dawned in his eyes. 'This is why you can't cut the strings on Jessie now...'

It wasn't a question.

'Old habits die hard, I guess. But when she met Adam, I thought she was set. He seemed like a nice guy, she had a good job in London, everything seemed kind of perfect and I lowered my guard. Then Mum's accident happened, and Jessie was amazing. She raced in, offering to take care of Mum, leaving her job to move back home so that I could keep mine. And I went along with it. I was worried about Mum, we both knew there could be no happy ending, but to see Jessie take control. She was wonderful, Brendan, and I was so proud... Of course, Adam turned out to be a complete tosser—'

His eyes widened, his head jerked up.

'Sorry. A waste of space, better?'

'I think pregnancy has you losing your filter.'

'Pregnancy or you. I think it's more likely to be you.'

He grinned. 'I'm not sure how to take that.'

'As a compliment, I guess. There aren't many people I truly speak my mind around.'

'So… Adam showed his true colours and…?'

'He broke up with her. Her panic attacks returned but she hid them from me. I was staying in the run-up to Mum's funeral and we had to go and visit the undertaker. He asked if we'd like to see Mum one last time and she wouldn't move, couldn't breathe. It was awful, Brendan. It was like all that progress over the years had gone, she was back to being that lost teenager again and I… I felt so helpless…'

He reached across the table, touched a hand to hers and the reassuring warmth spread through her.

'You can't put it all on you, Han. As a child your mother should have been there more.'

'Oh, she was when she was home. She was the one that comforted Jessie with her night terrors, she was the one who was quick to bring the hot milk and the cuddles. And she already blamed herself enough for everything, choosing a man like my dad, failing to give us a consistent father figure. She didn't get that all we really needed was her.'

He nodded. 'What happened after you'd seen the undertaker? Did you have it out with Jess?'

'I did and she admitted they'd returned with Mum's accident, the realisation that we're just pawns really, that we don't have full control over what happens to us. Like the person driving the car that hit Mum, they didn't know they were going to hit black ice and lose control. Like Mum when she popped out that day to go to the shops, she didn't know that if she'd only left five minutes earlier, later, whatever, she'd still be here now. And so, Jessie started seeing danger in everything and she didn't want to worry me. Me or Mum. She said she had the attacks under control, and I gave her the benefit of the doubt, but then the other week, not long before I came to see you in New York…'

Her cheeks flamed, her fingers twitching beneath his hand and he lifted it away, realising where her head was at and taking him there too.

'She had another. She was supposed to come and meet me at the station and I found her in the living room, surrounded by Mum's things, her head between her legs. She'd gone to leave and been hit by a tirade of what-ifs. What if my train had crashed? What if the brakes in the car failed? What if a lorry broke through the central reservation…? Honestly, she was pondering every bad situation at a million miles an hour and it was out of control. I arranged for her to see a counsellor, get some real help, and she's been going, but still…'

'Still, you worry?'

'Yes.'

She looked to her phone that was on the kitchen

side. 'Do you think if we just keep on at them, they'll behave?'

'Jessie and Joel—we can hope.'

'But you doubt it?'

'Without being there, who can know?'

She continued to stare at the phone.

'If it will make you feel better, we can fly out there towards the end of her break and you can see her for yourself. Give her some time, some freedom and then join her. It'll be a good chance for you to tell her the truth about Leon and the baby, away from here and the pressures of work. The break might do you good too, not to mention the sun.'

'We?'

'Yes.'

'You can get away from work?'

'If you can?'

Just as it had been for Jessie, it was an offer she couldn't refuse. 'I'd like that.'

'Then it's settled.'

She eyed him across the table, her heart all warm, her head all fuzzy. He really was the kindest, most thoughtful, most generous…

His eyes narrowed. 'What?'

'You.'

'What about me?'

'You're a special kind of guy, Brendan Hart.' It came out honest, heartfelt, a rasp, and his throat bobbed as the rest of his body seemed to still. 'One of a kind.'

'How so?' he asked, carefully.

'You're thoughtful, caring, giving, protective beyond measure… I wonder whether it's genetic and our child will be like you.'

He gave a soft chuckle. 'I'd like to say it was down to my upbringing, but my parents spent so much time working and travelling I was often in the care of a nanny or away at boarding school.'

'You didn't see them much?'

'We had time together in the summer and at Christmas. They were my happiest memories as a child.'

'But you'd rather have been with them more?'

'Is it that obvious?'

'It's written in your face…'

'Like you, I would have liked to have had a more normal childhood, yes…' He went quiet, his expression shifting with his thoughts, an internal battle only he was privy to.

'What is it?'

He leaned forward in his seat, his sudden intensity making her wary. 'I've been thinking about childcare.'

'You have?'

And why was she so surprised? This was Brendan, who'd been thinking of everything, and she'd already admitted to thinking about it herself. Didn't mean she was ready to talk about it though…

'I know it's early days but I don't want them being brought up by a stranger.'

'After what happened to you?'

'Possibly. Probably.'

'So, what are you saying?' She lifted her water to take a soothing sip.

'I know how important your job is to you and if you want to work full-time then I'm happy to pick up the slack.'

'The slack?' She choked on her drink. Its coolness doing nothing to ease the rising heat within, or the sudden thud of her heart in her chest. 'The slack' was her inability to be a good mother, a good parent…loving and enough. 'Because you'd make a better parent than me?'

'What? No!' His frown was sharp, his body rigid. 'That's not what I'm saying. You mentioned a live-in nanny and I'm saying I don't want that. And slack wasn't the best choice of words, but you know what I mean.'

She placed her glass down, careful not to let the tremor in her body show. It was true; he hadn't said it, she had. Because it was what she feared, it was what she believed.

'You're offering to be a stay-at-home dad?'

'It's quite normal in this day and age.'

'Normal, yes, but for us?'

She'd just assumed, with their schedules, that

they'd have a nanny, a childminder, someone…
a neutral party doing the nurturing, covering up
for her failings.

'Why not? I don't need the money, and I can
readily reduce my caseload.'

'You'd be pressured into giving up partner.'

'Perhaps.'

Brendan, a stay-at-home dad. She'd been worried about bonding with her baby before, but if
Brendan were to be the primary carer, their child
would live with him. Any custody battle would
always land in his favour, wherever he decided to
settle long term, their child would go too.

'Doesn't it bother you?' she asked, trying to ignore the crushing force within as she focused on
the partnership, the job, the one thing she could
vocalise.

'Not particularly.'

'Are you serious?'

'Never more…'

She felt light-headed, far too hot. Why hadn't
the thought occurred to her? There was no denying he'd be great at it, so much better than she
could ever hope to be, so why was it tearing her
apart inside? Why wasn't she glad of the offer?

It made the most sense. Practically. Emotionally. It gave stability for their child and her life
would continue. Her work-life balance untouched.

But her head was spinning, her mind trying
to paint a picture that she refused to accept…her

baby living somewhere else. Apart from her. In Brendan's arms. His look of love, of adoration, of her watching in from the outside, disconnected, unable to fit in. Alone.

But maybe things were better that way, maybe the baby was better off as far away from her broken self as possible.

Brendan knew what he was doing. Brendan could love them openly. Brendan could…he was…

'It makes a lot of sense, don't you think?'

'I hadn't— I don't—' She pushed herself up to standing, unable to meet his eye, unable to think straight. 'Pudding?'

She stepped away, she needed to catch her breath, she needed time to regroup and work out how she felt. This was too…it was all too much.

'Hannah?'

She swayed, her hand reaching for the table to steady herself, but it evaded her grasp. The fuzziness spread, her vision narrowing as he shifted on her periphery, his voice a distant echo. 'Hannah?'

She really was hot. She should've changed out of her jumper. She shouldn't have eaten quite so much. She shouldn't have—shouldn't have—

'Hannah?'

And then there was nothing.

CHAPTER ELEVEN

ONE MINUTE SHE was standing and the next she was in his arms, a dead weight.

'Hannah?'

He lowered her to the floor, telling himself to stay calm when his heart was screaming at him to do something. She was too hot, her skin all clammy. How had he not noticed? He *should* have noticed.

He laid her head in his lap, tugged out his phone. A quick search and he knew what to do: laying her on her left side, he pulled her knee to her chest and smoothed her hair back. Two minutes. He was to give her two minutes, but his fingers hovered ready to—

She stirred in his arms, her lashes fluttering...

'Hannah! Thank God, Hannah!'

'Brendan?' Her eyes opened, her face creased up and voice so small.

'I'm here, baby, I'm here.'

'What—what happened?'

'You fainted.'

The lines across her brow deepened, her hand pushing into the floor as she tried to sit up.

'Oh, no, you don't. Not yet.'

'But I'm fine.'

She didn't sound fine. She sounded far too frail, and he cursed himself for not doing something sooner.

Like what? You're not psychic. You couldn't have known.

She didn't fight him as he pulled her head to his lap and continued to stroke the hair from her face. She still looked deathly pale, her lips blue, and somewhere deep his heart was still struggling to regain a normal rhythm. Guilt gnawing at his insides.

He shouldn't have brought up childcare. The look on her face when she'd accused him of believing he'd make the better parent...the pain, the panic, the loss. It wasn't about being better, it was about her thinking that she wasn't good enough. And it crushed him.

'I'm not sure what happened. I was getting pudding and then...'

'And then you fainted.'

'But I never faint...'

'Shh, Hannah, just lie still for a while.'

At least until he saw some colour back in her face and he was certain she was okay.

'But I'm fine,' she repeated.

'Do you normally faint?'

'No.'

'Then it's not fine.'

'I'm sure it's just a freak occurrence.'

He lifted his phone once more, checked over the rest of the page.

She shifted in his lap. 'What are you doing?'

'I'm Googling it.'

'I thought you told me you couldn't trust everything you read.'

'As far as celeb gossip goes, but the NHS helpline I trust.'

She went quiet, leaving him to his reading, which was a good job because he needed the peace to calm his pulse and he didn't want any of his panic leaching into her.

'Satisfied yet?'

'How are you feeling now?'

'Fine.' She did sound stronger, more like Hannah. 'But if you keep making me repeat myself that's going to change.'

'Why is it so hard for you to lie still?'

She hid beneath her lashes, her cheeks colouring. The sign of vitality filling him with relief... until he realised where her head was resting and the reason she was blushing and his lower body came alive.

Move.

'I'll get you a pillow.'

She wriggled upright as he freed her. 'I'd rather get to the sofa.'

'Of course...just take it slow.'

She avoided his eye as he walked her to the living area, her cheeks still pink as she settled back against the cushions.

'Better?' He scanned her face, looking for any sign she was about to go again. But she only looked self-conscious now.

'I feel such a fool.'

'Why?'

'For fainting.'

'*Feeling* like a fool is the foolish thing to do, it's hardly your fault. Do you want some water?'

'Please.'

He grabbed her glass from the dining table and offered it out to her.

'Thank you,' she murmured, head bowed.

'You can't be embarrassed, Han.'

'Next time you faint in front of me, I'll remind you of that.' She scraped an unsteady hand through her hair, reminding him of his own fingers doing the same, *wishing* they were still doing the same.

He sat down beside her and unlocked his phone screen, threw his attention into ticking off the health checklist.

'Do you feel any pain?'

'Unless you mean the pain of humiliation, no.'

'Do you still feel dizzy?'

She rolled her eyes. 'Brendan, please.'

'If you don't want me marching you to A & E right now, I suggest you humour me.'

She blew out a breath. 'No. Not any more.'

'Pain in your chest? Shortness of breath?'

'No.'

'Is your vision okay?'

'Yes.'

'Do you have a headache?'

She turned to look at him.

'Apart from me?'

Her eyes sparkled. 'No.'

'Good. And lastly…'

He turned to her and lifted his hand to her neck, she backed away, raised her hand to block his, her eyes wide. 'What are you doing?'

'I'm checking your pulse.'

Her throat bobbed. 'What do you know about…?'

'I know enough. Now sit still and be a good patient.'

She went rigid, her eyes fixed on his, and he smoothed his hand beneath the fabric of her polo neck, tried to ignore the way her lips parted, her eyes dilated, the way her skin felt beneath his touch…

He found her pulse, the regular beat a reassurance in itself, and then he tracked the second hand on his watch and started to count.

'Brendan, I really think—'

'Shh.' He lifted his eyes to hers, read the burn residing there. 'I'm counting.'

He began again…counting as the contact thrummed through him. Lost track and tried again. Nothing to do with her resistance or interference now and everything to do with the contact, the subtle beat of her heart, the look in her eyes and he closed his own.

He forced himself to concentrate and breathed a sigh of relief when he calculated a steady seventy-two beats a minute. All good.

He opened his eyes to tell her but the look in her face had him stalling… 'Hannah?'

She swallowed, her voice a husky rasp. 'Are you done?'

He dropped his hand back, sensing her urgency wrapped up in the chemistry, and he gave an abrupt nod. 'You're all good. But maybe you should—' he cleared his throat '—go to the bathroom and check all is okay.'

She looked at him oddly.

'I think I'd know.'

He wet his lips. 'Okay. But I think we should get an appointment to see your midwife first thing Monday.'

'Because?'

'She needs to know what happened just in case there's anything more to it.'

'Like?'

'I don't know, Han. It's not uncommon to experience dizzy spells in the first trimester, but I'd rather you got checked out professionally.'

'So why are you still scowling?'

'Is there someone you can call to come and stay with you?'

'What, right now?'

He nodded and she pressed him away. 'Don't be silly, Brendan, I don't need someone to watch over me.'

'And what if I hadn't been here? What if you'd hit your head? Fallen down some stairs? Did yourself and the baby a real injury, what then?'

She shook her head, but the colour seeped from her cheeks.

'You know I'm right.'

'But seriously…'

'I'm going to stay the night. I can take the sofa if you—'

'Don't be ridiculous!'

'Hannah, I'm not going to fight with you on this. Jessie is away and if there's no one else you can call, I'm staying.'

'I just got up too fast, that's all!'

'You can't know that for sure and save your breath, because I'm not going to change my mind. I won't be happy until you've been checked out professionally.'

She stared back at him, her thoughts racing, her eyes quivering with every unreadable one and he waited for her to come to the same conclusion—the *only* conclusion.

'What about tomorrow?'

'We'll take each day as it comes, but you can stay at my place.' He stood to create some distance between them, sensing their proximity wasn't helping, and listed off the practical. 'I have plenty of room,

I'm closer to work, the hospital and the midwife. And you can have as much space as you need.'

She looked up at him, eyes wide. 'You want us to move in together?'

'Yes.'

'Until I've seen the midwife, or…'

He knew her thoughts had travelled in the same direction. 'Until we know this really is a one-off.'

'And how long before we can possibly know that?'

'However long it takes, Hannah. I'm the father of this baby. I'm responsible for the two of you and if you think I'm going to leave you on your own after what just happened, then you don't know me very well at all.'

'Brendan, what's up?'

Brendan spun away from the hospital doors and cursed down the phone. 'Where the hell are you, Leon?'

'I'm in Chicago, working on the Owens' case.'

'You're supposed to be on the plane. I told Sally to—'

'And I told your PA I don't need your private jet. Thanks for the offer, though.'

'For God's sake, her mum's in Intensive Care, Leon. It doesn't look good. Sending you that plane was my way of getting you back here as soon as possible.'

'I get on that plane and I kiss my chance at being made partner goodbye.'

'We're talking about your mother-in-law's life, Leon, not some case that can wait!'

'That's easy for you to say when you're already partner, mate.'

'Leon, I mean it. Get on that blasted plane and get yourself to Hannah's side. Or so help me...'

'So help you what?'

Good question. There was no answer he could give. The silence was punctuated by the monitors beeping in the background, the gentle weeping of Jessie as Hannah held her. He turned to look at them through the glass, his arms aching to go to her.

'She needs you here, Leon.'

The guy gave a tight laugh. 'She doesn't need me, Brendan. That woman needs no one.'

'You're talking about your wife.'

'That's right. So believe me when I say she'll be fine. I have to go.'

The phone went dead and Brendan stared daggers at it.

Was Leon serious?

Yes, Hannah was tough. But this...this was enough to break even her, and he wasn't willing to let that happen.

'Brendan?'

He turned and there she was, stoic, her eyes on the phone in his hand, but her voice was quiet, so very quiet.

'Was that Leon?'

He nodded. 'He...he's stuck in Chicago.'

She looked over her shoulder, back through the doors to where Jessie now sipped at a hot drink.

'How's she holding up?'

Her eyes came back to him, and he saw the slightest tremor in her lower lip.

'As well as can be expected.'

'How about you?'

She swallowed, lifted her chin with a rapid nod.

'Hannah?'

'Hmm...?'

'Come here.'

He opened his arms.

There was a second's delay and then she stepped into his hold, her body sagging against him. She didn't cry. She didn't need to. He could sense her world crumbling and knew he'd be there to help piece it back together.

'Thank you, Brendan. Thank you for being here.'

'Always...'

He kissed her hair, held her to him, uncaring whether it was crossing a line, uncaring about anything but the woman in his arms.

'I'll always be here for you, Hannah.'

CHAPTER TWELVE

'*HOWEVER LONG IT TAKES, HANNAH...*'

There was no doubt in her mind as she stared up at him, her heart doing a wild dance in her chest, that he meant it.

Her feet itched to run...until her head reminded her that this was her home. Not his.

If anyone was leaving, it was him.

Not that he would, he'd made that abundantly clear.

She breathed through the fluttering in her chest, tried to keep her thoughts rational...

Good sense told her he was right. What if she had fallen and hurt herself, or, worse, hurt the baby?

But good sense also told her this wasn't safe. Not in the physical, she-didn't-trust-him way. Never that. But in the emotional, she-could-get-hooked-on-this kind of a way and she was already susceptible enough. To him, to the way he made her feel, the way her heart and thoughts fired off in all directions and made clear decision-making impossible.

'You haven't got any clothes with you, any toiletries...'

'That's easily rectified.'

He was typing on his phone again and she felt as if she were living through some out-of-body experience watching down as this happened to somebody else. Or maybe that was the after-effect of the episode that had landed her in this mess?

'Done. My driver will have a bag here within the hour. Is there anything he can fetch for you en route? Food, drink, anything?'

'No. No, I think—I think I need the bathroom.' She went to stand and he was there in a panicked heartbeat, his palm soft beneath her elbow, the other reaching to her waist, and she jerked away.

'Sorry, did I hurt you?'

'No.' Not that she could tell him the truth, that every time he touched her, her entire body pulsed with it. Need. Want. An emotion she couldn't put a lid on but felt far too close to affection...to love.

She shifted out of his hold, hid her eyes from him. 'I can get there under my own steam, Brendan. I'll call if I need you.'

She knew he wasn't convinced, his concern evident as he agitated to follow. 'You can hardly call if you—'

'And what's the other option?' She dared to meet his eye in her frustration, desperation. 'You're going to come with me and watch me pee? I really don't think so.'

His cheeks warmed, enhancing the molten quality to his chocolate-brown eyes—she *loved* chocolate. Loved it all the more since she'd become pregnant. The rich, soothing goodness, the sweet naughtiness of it, too…much like the man standing before her…

'I'll be right back.'

She raced rather than walked, his deep baritone following close behind. 'I'll be right outside the door.'

The door that she promptly locked and dropped to the floor against, her eyes on the ceiling, her head and heart racing. How had she got here? How could it all have gone so wrong?

Everything had been perfect three years ago. She was on track to make senior partner. Mum had been fit and well. Jessie had been settled with Adam in London. She and Leon had been… Okay, she'd *thought* she and Leon were perfect, or at least happy in their arrangement, blissful in her ignorance.

Now her life plan was in tatters. No mum. No marriage. No stability.

The only thing she had left of it was her job but for how long? She didn't want her child living separately from her. She didn't want to be an absentee mother. She didn't want to fail them. But how could she have it all and not spread herself too thinly?

How could she let Brendan step up while she stepped down? How could she bring a life into the world when she didn't even know how to love? How to give herself over so completely? What if it wasn't something you could learn? What if she shut down even more? What if—?

The gentle rap on the door had her jerking forward, her panicked gaze on the handle.

'You okay in there?'

She swallowed. Hardly. Her life was so unrecognisable as her own, she feared she'd start rocking any second and then what would Brendan do? Wrap his arms around her. Comfort her. Make her need him. Make her crave him.

And she didn't mean sexually. She meant emotionally. Offering her security, support, safety.

And no one had ever given her that. Not her parents. Not her husband. She'd learned from a very young age that the only person you could depend on to give you that was yourself. She'd shared her life with Leon, but she'd never *depended* on him for those things.

If anyone had played the alpha, it had been her and that had been fine. Perfectly fine. Because she'd been the one in control. Of their life, her emotions, everything…

But Brendan…she had no walls when it came to him.

No protection. No control.

And now he was insisting, swearing an oath even, to look after her. To stand by her. To give her all that she'd once given herself. And she'd never felt so high. So warm and cherished. And utterly, utterly terrified.

'Hannah?' He tried the door handle. *'Hannah?'*

Why couldn't she find her voice? Why couldn't she tell him she was okay?

The lock beneath the handle turned as he opened it from the other side and she scurried back from the moving door.

'Hannah?' So much softer now as he froze in the doorway and took her in. 'Oh, Hannah.'

He was on the floor in a heartbeat, pulling her against him.

'It'll be okay, baby. It will.'

She was shaking all over. 'It won't, Brendan. It won't! I don't know what I'm doing. I don't know how to be a good mum. I don't know how to love a child. What if I can't do it? What if they grow to hate me? What if I'm not enough? What if they—they—?'

'Shh, baby, shh… It'll be okay. I promise. They're not going to hate you.' He rocked her with his words, hugged her tighter. 'They're going to love you. I promise.'

'You can't know that.' She was still shaking. 'You can't.'

'I know you and I know enough. And you're not doing this alone. I've got you. I've always got you.'

But how long for?

Until she failed their child. Until her cold-hearted ways pushed both him and their child away…

Leon's voice permeated the panicked haze. *'Thank God you never wanted children, Hannah, because that heart of yours has no space for anyone but yourself.'*

'What if I can't love them, Brendan?' she whispered.

He quit rocking and pressed her away from him, his palms on either side of her face as he met her gaze, and the blazing intensity in his eyes stole her breath away.

'How can you ask that when everything you've done, you've done for your sister and your mother, your family, for love?'

Her lashes fluttered, her vision blurring with her tears. 'But I'm scared, Brendan.'

'It's okay to be scared, to be fearful of the unknown.' He brought her forehead to his lips, took a breath as he kissed her gently. 'It would be strange if you weren't, but we've got this, Hannah. Together, we will get it right.'

Together... That was what she was afraid of.

She folded into him, stared at the wall ahead.

Together meant depending on him, opening herself up to him, needing him and where would her control be then?

In tatters, just as it is now...

CHAPTER THIRTEEN

'SEE, I TOLD you everything would be fine.'

Brendan struggled to hear her over the hurried clip of her heels echoing through the underground car park. She was half a stride ahead of him, a position she seemed to have adopted ever since her breakdown Saturday night.

A breakdown he could almost believe had never happened.

'Doesn't it feel better to have had the midwife tell you that though?'

She harrumphed but he knew her too well, he saw the way her shoulders had lowered just a fraction, the small breath that had escaped her lips when the midwife had confirmed that all looked normal. She could pretend all she liked, but he knew.

She jabbed the button for his private lift. Jabbed it again when it failed to light.

'Here, allow me…' He reached in front of her, his arm lightly brushing across her front as he swiped his access card over the reader before pressing the button, his every sense attuned to her…the subtle inhalation that had her chin tilting up, the rigid posture. Was it the sweeping contact or was it her frustration that she sensed he saw through her?

The doors opened and she stepped inside, turned to stare at the doors as he entered beside her.

'I'll arrange for you to have a separate key card. Charles knows that you're staying with me so any problems, you can reach out to him. I'll send you his mobile number.'

The lift doors slid quietly closed and she nodded in acknowledgement but didn't look at him. Not even for the briefest of moments. She held her briefcase in both hands before her. Her ponytail as smooth and as glossy as it had been that morning. Her make-up pristine. Her head still sporting that distinctive, confident tilt. They might as well be at work, the opposing counsel in the same elevator. The distance she was creating so very marked. The superiority too.

And yet, it felt so very forced, and he was sick of it. The front, the pretence, didn't she know she could be herself with him? The only time she'd truly been herself had been that night, when she'd thrown off the cloak and succumbed to the chemistry between them.

And he wanted that Hannah back. Burned with the urge to pull her up against his chest and kiss her until she gave him the real her, the unrestrained her... Heat pulsed through him as he recollected that night, her perfume crossing the confined space in real time and compounding its effect over his body...hard and aching and *dammit all*, she wasn't his to have.

The lift doors opened and he shoved good manners aside as he strode into his apartment, throwing down his case and slackening off his tie. He headed for his drinks cabinet, then he remembered, she couldn't drink.

Mentally cursing, he did an about-turn and headed for the kitchen instead, undoing the top button of his shirt as she followed close behind. He blew out a breath as he scoured the cupboards for inspiration.

'Tired?' She flicked a look in his direction, her eyes narrowing just enough to show she cared before she looked away again.

'A little.'

Liar. You're hyped up and good for a burn-out session in the gym...or in bed with her. The former was a possibility, the latter was a risky venture. Hands down, he knew which one he'd prefer.

'I'm sorry. When they offered me the late appointment after work, I just took it. Maybe it would have been better to—'

'No. It was right to take the appointment. Hopefully we can both get some sleep now. Less of the worry.'

She glanced in his direction, too brief for him to make contact. And he wanted to. He wanted to look her right in the eye and read her like the book she'd always been to him. But it felt as though that book was closing with each passing day...

How was it possible to get to know someone more and gradually lose that insight?

'Can I get you a drink?' He pulled out the menus for the select local restaurants he trusted to deliver a decent meal and slid them across the marble worktop to her. 'You can pick whatever you like for dinner...'

'Do you have any green tea?'

'If it was on the grocery list you gave me, then yes, I will.' He opened the sleek black cupboard above the counter that was now filled with items he didn't recognise, labels facing neatly to the front. His housekeeper, Joyce, was worth her weight in gold. 'One green tea coming up.'

'Do you mind if I change?'

'Not at all.' He tapped the kettle on and dropped a teabag into her mug, gesturing to the menus. 'Do you know what you fancy?'

'To be honest, something simple...'

'Like?'

She shrugged. 'An omelette?'

'An omelette? Really?'

'With some salad maybe.'

'That's all you want?'

'Please.'

'But the Thai is excellent?'

'And right now, I don't think I can stomach it.'

'Okay.' He nodded, careful not to ask her what was wrong. He knew that question was grating on her, especially when the answer was often the same—*morning sickness is just a label and a very poor descriptor, you men have no idea.* 'You have the bedroom straight down the hall, its adjoining bathroom should have everything you need. Joyce unpacked your things today but if there's anything you can't find, just let me know.'

She nodded, her fingers worrying the back of her neck.

'She should be here before we leave in the morning. I can introduce you then.'

She nodded some more, fingers still twitching, eyes roaming around the room.

'Are you okay?'

Dammit. He clamped his teeth together. *You weren't supposed to ask.*

'Doesn't this feel a little odd to you?'

Relieved he hadn't got her back up, he gave the hint of a smile. 'Having spent two nights at your place, this doesn't feel all that different.'

The kettle clicked off and he poured hot water into her mug, his words coming with his thoughts. 'I'll start looking for somewhere new on the commuter line after the baby comes. It'll be nice to have a garden, somewhere they can run wild and have fun. Slides, swings, a playhouse. I always wanted one of those cars, you know, the red and yellow one with the squeaky horn and the pedals to make it move.'

Her eyes were wide and fixed on the drink as he stirred it, a telltale sheen appearing but she blinked it away just as quick. 'Baby steps, okay?'

'Baby steps.' He passed her the mug, knowing he'd got carried away, but he could hardly take it back, not when it was true.

'Do you think I could take a bath?'

'Now?'

She gave him a weak smile. 'If it's no trouble...'

'Of course... *mi casa es su casa.*'

Dear God, he was throwing Spanish platitudes at her. Who was more awkward now?

'Thanks.'

'Anything else you need?'

Her lashes lifted, colour rising in her cheeks as she shook her head.

'I'll get on with the omelette. Want anything special in it? Jalapeños, olives, pineapple...'

'Are you listing my pizza order at me?'

'A craving's a craving, right?'

Her lips twisted into the closest thing to an authentic smile he'd seen in days. 'A bit of cheese and chilli would be great.'

'As you w—' Her brows nudged up and he swiftly changed it up. 'I'm on it.'

He watched her go, his heart joining his foot in his mouth.

Every time he saw her vulnerable, it chipped away at the walls he had built up.

Walls that were there to prevent him from falling in deep.

Walls that were there as a reality check. Her on one side, very much pregnant with his child, still married to another man and with a heart that he could never claim.

And him on the other, his love unrequited but no less true.

And what he couldn't do was hope. Hope that one day she would cross over and return it. That one day she would love him as wholly as he loved her.

His gaze drifted to the whisky shining gold in his cabinet and he turned away.

Drink wasn't the answer.

But what was?

'Thank you so much for coming with me!'

Hannah reached up on tiptoes, kissed Brendan's cheek in greeting, and for a split second the world stilled and his heart stopped.

'You'd think after a decade I'd know what to buy Leon for his thirtieth but I'm floundering.'

And you'd think after a decade he'd be able to take a peck from her without his entire body going into overdrive.

She dropped back, eyed the takeaway coffees in his hand. 'One of those for me?' She cocked

her head at him. 'Hello? Earth to Brendan...'
She waved a hand in front of his face, her cheeks
aglow, eyes alive. 'Anybody home?'

'Sorry.' He shook himself awake, handed her a
cup. 'That Rochester case is a total distraction.'

She grimaced. 'I'm sorry...it really does have
the media in a frenzy too, doesn't it? Are you
okay? We really don't need to do this now if you
would rather get back to it.'

'No, I need the break. I can't read another de-
position without seeing double...'

'A sure sign that you do need to get out. I'll
make it worth your while, I promise.'

There were so many ways she could make it
worth his while...none of them professional and
all of them forbidden...

He started to move, striding down the sidewalk.

'I can give you some time, if need be,' she offered, tucking her arm into his. 'A fresh eye and
all that. I'm in New York for the next fortnight so
I'm around.'

And that extra eye was worth a hundred when
it came to Hannah. There was a reason she was
the firm's highest billing lawyer, with her advice
sought by its many offices across the globe. And
if it meant extra time together...

'That would be great.'

'And don't worry. I'll ensure Leon and I return
the favour and buy you an amazing thirtieth gift
too.' She gave him a wink. 'So where shall we

head first? I keep meaning to take a proper tour of the place...it's such an impressive city. I can see why you chose to practise here over London.'

'It's okay, I guess.'

'Okay? Wow! Such high praise...'

He chuckled, then looked away before she could spy the truth. He'd chosen to practise in New York because it had put distance between him and her and Leon. It had nothing to do with the appeal of the city and everything to do with the appeal of her.

'So, where do we start?'

'Start?'

'The present-hunt! Are you sure you don't want to get back to work...?'

'What about Harvey's? Leon had his eye on some cufflinks there the other week...'

'Cufflinks...' She nodded. 'I like your thinking... though his cufflink collection could contend with my shoe collection—don't you think he already has enough?'

'You know Leon. He likes to look the part. Can't be caught at a function wearing the same ones twice.'

She frowned. 'If I'm getting them from Harvey's he'd better wear them more.'

'Which brings me to budget... How much do you want to spend?'

'Enough to make him feel special...not so much that if he does only dust them off once I regret it.'

He chuckled. 'Fair enough.'

'I just want to make sure it's special. The Nutcracker was such a thoughtful gift. Mum and Jessie loved it too, and getting to spend that time with
them meant so much.'

He murmured his response, smothering the
truth that for her thirtieth she'd almost ended up
with nothing. That the grand tier box tickets for
the Royal Opera House to see The Nutcracker had
been his idea, his purchase. December being the
month of her birthday and her love of ballet making it the perfect choice.

It wasn't as if he'd ever envisaged going with
her. The tickets had been for her to take whom-
ever she chose. And if Leon hadn't visited him
that day and caught sight of the tickets he'd pur-
chased...if he hadn't ribbed him mercilessly for
seducing some unsuspecting woman and forcing
himself to endure two hours of 'prancing', perhaps he wouldn't have handed them over as a
back-up gift on the off-chance that Leon had forgotten her big birthday was fast approaching.

And it didn't matter that Hannah didn't know
the truth, because the important thing was she'd
got to go and she'd got to go with her family, who
she rarely saw enough of.

It was a vicious circle—she worked to support
her family, but work was the thing that also took
her away, and with that gift he'd given her back
a piece of sacred time.

It wasn't much, but it was enough.

CHAPTER FOURTEEN

HANNAH WAS ACCUSTOMED to fancy hotels, the firm being nothing but generous in permitting them the best when it came to accommodation and wining and dining clients.

And she and Leon had never scrimped on the few holidays they had taken.

But Brendan's penthouse was on another level. The bedroom she'd been assigned had the same exposed brick outer wall and honey oak floor as the main living area, though here the roofline sloped either side of an impressive circular window criss-crossed with the same steel. She could imagine, come morning, the sun casting cubes of golden light over the bed beneath…

The huge, seriously inviting bed that looked as if it possessed a fluffy white cloud for a duvet, a mountain of pillows and a plush cream throw. Her gaze narrowed as she scanned the rest of the room. The cream wingback chair with its coordinating footstool and cushion, the rugs either side of the bed, the ivory flowers on the dressing table. All soft, neutral colours.

All *her* colours.

He might as well have lifted her flat's interior decor and plonked it here. The only difference was the industrial backdrop of the mill, but it worked. It seriously worked.

It also made her heart take a tiny leap, her stomach too.

He'd done this. In the two days he'd had to sort it, he'd arranged this. Given her a home from home...

'Joyce unpacked your things today...'

She placed her drink on a slate coaster next to the bed and strode up to the folding doors in one wall. Taking a breath, she slid them ajar and couldn't contain her gasp. The fully fitted dressing room was the size of her flat's bedroom. More flowers adorned the centre island that had drawers on all sides and a glass top under which the accessories she'd chosen to bring were meticulously laid out. All three surrounding walls were a combination of rails, drawers, shelves—her belongings meticulously folded or pressed on hangers, her shoes, boots, handbags neatly arranged.

It was exquisite...and it didn't feel like the guest room at all. It had the air of the master. But it couldn't be.

Brendan might have transported her life and her personal tastes here, but he wouldn't give her his room. This was a not so subtle reminder that though they were both wealthy and equal when it came to their partner status, he was still very much a billionaire with a huge hotel empire beneath him. He could afford a place in the city that was filled with rooms like this one.

She touched a hand to her stomach, her whispered words for their child alone. 'You'll never want for anything, darling, that much I can tell you now.'

Not as she had wanted.

Not as she'd worked night and day to get her grades and bring in what money she could while Mum had done her thing, tried to be all present while forever chasing her latest love.

Brendan's vision of the future came back to her unawares, tears pricking with its poignant perfection. His mention of a home with a playground for a garden had swiftly morphed into a picture of them enjoying it, the three of them, a picture-perfect family, only that wasn't what they were. And the realisation crushed her as quickly as his vision had warmed her.

For an awful moment she'd thought she was going to break down again, sink to the floor as she had last Saturday and weep her heart out like a fool.

How could she have done that? Looked so weak, so broken in front of him. It turned her stomach even now. She'd never looked that weak in front of anyone, not Jessie, not Mum and certainly not Leon.

But here she was again, breaking down in front

of him, always him. And she had to stop it. She was to be a mother, for goodness' sake, her child would need her to be the strong one…but not too strong. Disciplined but not severe. Loving but not indulgent. And so on, her uncertain brain wanted to ramble and she shook her head, desperate to empty it as she returned to the bedroom.

Get a bath, get your head straightened out, and then—

Her phone buzzed in her pocket and frowning, she pulled it out, instantly relieved to see a message from Jessie. She'd heard nothing since the apology she'd sent the previous night…

I know you're only trying to protect me, but I know what I'm doing. I promise. xx

She stared at the message, the tears making a swift return as she tried to type a response, but nothing would come. Nothing that wouldn't aggravate things further. And the truth was, who was she to judge when her life was in such turmoil?

She threw the phone on the bed, her words muttered into the ether, 'If you could only see me now, Jessie, you wouldn't believe it for a second.'

She unbuttoned her blouse and headed for the only other doors in the room. She pushed them open and her aching limbs sighed over the spa-like serenity before her. The seductive mix of rich wood, dark tile, and copper accents, a his and her sink and a glass-walled shower that would fit a family of five. A sunken bath that would fit them all too. And a scent in the air that begged you to close your eyes and breathe it in.

She set the waterfall tap over the bath running and turned around, spying the dressing gown hooked on the back of the door. Was that for her to use?

She fingered the soft white fabric, brought it to her nose. It smelled clean and fresh and comforting…until she realised why. It was Brendan. Whatever detergent his staff—Joyce?—used, it was all him. And her body *liked* it.

Was that the baby? Some innate response? Or had it always existed, like that day they'd first met, when she'd known he was different, that he was special, he was—?

And now you sound just like Jessie!

She swiftly dropped the sleeve and concentrated on what she was supposed to be doing—taking that bath—but even as she lay in the water, several minutes later, hair washed, body clean, she couldn't shift the sensation. His presence working some kind of magic over her, making her body prickle and warm. The swirling heat in her abdomen, nothing to do with her bath and everything to with him.

She'd Googled it after their eventful dinner together. She understood that the increased blood flow through pregnancy meant greater arousal, increased sensitivity and a libido to match. She could explain it all away as just another symptom. Only it wasn't that easy. Not when she wanted it. Wanted him. And now she was living with him.

The one man that could turn her on with a simple look, a simple touch, a simple… She threw her hands in the air with a groan as she accepted he could read her a children's book and she'd likely be a panting, aching mess, begging him to give her some release.

And she knew he could. Knew too well how skilled he was and her body shivered with the thrill, the memory, the idea of more…

She covered her face with her hands. But this was Brendan—Brendan! The closest thing she had to a best friend and now the father of her child. She couldn't let things get out of hand any more than they already had…no matter what her hyped-up and very pregnant body was trying to tell her.

But when he looked like he had tonight, his dark hair ruffled with concern, his tie slackened off, shirt unbuttoned at the collar, his rich, masculine scent, warm from the exertions of the day… She'd been a hot, needy mess. The car ride had been torture, the lift torture still and then to enter his penthouse, his private domain with him all rough around the edges and sexier than ever with it…

Curse her overexcited ovaries!

She sank beneath the water and wished she

could've had a wine, rather than a tea. She'd have stayed submerged too if it weren't for an almighty noise that ripped through the entire building and rumbled through the bath.

She shot up, water sloshing over the sides as her head darted this way and that.

Was that—? Was that the *fire alarm*?

No, it couldn't be, but…

But it was!

She scrambled out, throwing a towel around herself as she legged it from the room…

'Brendan! What on earth are you—?'

Brandishing a flapping tea towel, he turned and lost the ability to speak. Hannah, soaking wet and clinging the smallest of towels around her middle, was racing up to him, eyes as wild as the vibe she was giving off.

Holy Mother of…

Not that he could blame her—the fire alarm was still ringing, piercing his drums—but he couldn't string two words together in the face of her *nakedness*.

'Brendan?' She stopped just short of the kitchen, taking in the smoking pan he was currently wafting about as if it would somehow help while still fanning at the smoke alarm in the ceiling. 'Is that…dinner?'

'Was,' he shouted over the alarm, shoving the pan back on the hob.

He combed his fingers through his hair and held them there as he frowned down at the cremated remains and willed his body to chill. *Just don't turn around. Don't turn a—*

She came up behind him, peered over his shoulder to take in the delicacy he had created. 'Looks lovely.'

He grunted as the fire alarm finally quit, a blessed relief on his ears, the noise in other parts of his anatomy raging on. 'You sure you don't want takeaway?'

She giggled. 'And you had the gall to take the mick out of my cooking.'

'Why do you think I suggested buying food in?'

She started to laugh—a proper belly-tickling laugh—and it coaxed him into turning, coaxed him into looking at her, truly looking at her.

'What?' Her lips still danced, her eyes still shone, but the mood was shifting beneath them…

'I love hearing you laugh. It's been a while…'

A groove appeared between her brows. 'I laugh.'

'When?' Without thinking, he reached out to sweep a dripping wet strand behind her ear and found himself stuck there, his hand resting as he pressed, 'When was the last time you truly laughed like that?'

She caught her bottom lip in her teeth, her eyes wavering against his probing stare. 'There hasn't been a lot to laugh about of late.'

'No. But if I'd known burning some eggs would do it, I would have done it for you months ago.'

She opened her mouth but nothing came out. The air was thick, heavy, neither breaking the peace, neither moving…and he wanted to. He wanted to pull her to him, claim her parted lips, but he was too afraid he'd spook her. Too afraid she'd pack up her things and run when he'd only just got her here.

'Brendan, I…'

'Hannah, you?' He responded on autopilot and she stepped into him, her hands lifting to his hair. A second's delay as surprise gave way to sensation, to the towel slipping to the floor as her naked body pressed up against his and her eyes, hooded and pleading, locked with his.

'I want you,' she whispered against his lips.

He groaned, every fibre of his being revelling in the words, her actions. 'Are you sure about this, Hannah?'

'Never more.'

'But…'

Why are you still questioning it when she's all you've ever wanted?

'I'm done fighting this.'

What did that mean? Done fighting? When had she *started* fighting it? How long had she been fighting it? So many questions, and every one would break the mood he had no intention of breaking.

'You and me both.' And then he kissed her back as though his life depended on it, pressed her entire body against him and still it wasn't enough. He grabbed her by the hips and lifted her around him, backed her up to the kitchen surface as she tugged at his hair.

He was losing the power to breathe, to speak and she was panting, her legs taut as she rocked against him, the colour high in her chest and her cheeks.

She yanked his tie undone, wrapped it around her fists as she used it to anchor him close. Their kiss was wild, frenzied, their teeth clashing, chests heaving. He sensed she was close, the swift build-up surprising and intoxicating, feeding his own pleasure as she tore at his shirt next, buttons flying this way and that, and she gave a cursed apology.

'I don't care. I'll buy another.'

'I'll buy it for you.' She shoved his shirt from his shoulders and it caught on his wrists, hanging there as he brought her against his hardness, gave her the friction she craved and worshipped her moans.

'Brendan, I can't hold back—I can't—'

'Don't, baby, let go.'

'But I—I—'

The intercom buzzed through the room and they froze, tongues entangled, bodies entwined.

'*Damnit*, Charles…'

'The alarm?' she rasped.

He should have known the man would check in. It was his job to.

'If I don't answer he'll be up here in two.'

And that would mean her getting dressed and there was no way he wanted her clothed, no way he wanted to risk a reset on this. 'Don't move.'

Her cheeks flushed deeper, her nod a blessing and a curse. Because now she was naked on his kitchen counter and he had to make a call in sight. Temptation of the highest, most debilitating order.

He dragged a hand through his hair, released her though he loathed every separated inch. He unbuttoned his cuffs, threw his shirt to the ground and pressed the receiver. 'Sorry, Charles, false alarm. Thought I'd try my hand at cooking.'

He caught her eye, her pulse ticking wildly in her throat, her breasts that undulated with every rapid breath she took, and down further still…

'So, everything's okay, sir…sir?'

'Yes!' It came out far harsher than he intended. *Take a breath.* 'Everything save for the overdone eggs.'

Charles chuckled. Hannah's eyes danced. 'Very well, sir. Have a good evening.'

'Oh, I intend to.'

He was back upon her in a heartbeat, his hands in her hair, his inhalation sharp as he kissed her and breathed her in. Her legs resumed their hooked position, her moan illicit and undoing him from within.

'Tell me to stop and I will,' he rasped against her mouth, his hands shifting down her body. 'Tell me what you want, and I'll do that too.'

Because he would. He always would. It was as though he had been put on this earth with the sole purpose of worshipping this woman. At her side was where he found his peace, his pleasure and everything in between.

'I don't need to tell you, Brendan.' Her nails raked down his back. 'Because you already know.'

She couldn't have given his heart more pleasure and he groaned his response, dipping to catch one thrusting nipple between his teeth, and she cried out. He rolled her other between his thumb and forefinger, gently pinching, and she gripped him tighter.

'I mean it, Brendan.' She was so earnest, so desperate. 'I want you. Here. Now.'

He straightened, gazed down into her eyes that were so full of need there was no doubt in his mind that she meant it. And he wanted to treasure it, savour it.

It wasn't like that night in New York, tainted by Leon, tainted by her pain, by their betrayal too. This was something else. Deeper. Meaningful.

He stroked the hair back from her face, kissed her softly. 'I want you too.'

She lowered her hands to his belt buckle and

he didn't stop her. She held his eye as she looped it through and unfastened his trousers. Bit her lip as she palmed him, the slightest squeeze and he bucked, his curse an exhalation as he gripped her wrist.

'What's wrong?'

He struggled to take a breath, to speak. 'Just go easy.'

She frowned up at him, the flash of vulnerability in her eyes killing him. 'Did I do something wrong?'

'No. Hell, no. But I won't last another second if you keep up with that.'

Her sultry smile torched him, her palms easing around his hips as she smoothed away his briefs, his trousers with them. 'Well, when you put it like that… I like seeing you out of control. I like being responsible for it.'

She moved her hand over him and his body rocked in tune—it would be easy, too easy, to go with it. And he'd never been one for taking the easy road. Hannah had seen to that.

'You're not the only one.'

He dropped to his knees before she could stop him, his mouth covering her sensitised flesh, his tongue flicking over her. She was so ready for him, her taste, her need, all a drug that he couldn't get enough of. He teased her apart with his fingers and she bucked against him, her hands clawing at his hair as her breaths came thick and fast, his name too, and then she was juddering, her climax claiming her and flooding him with heat, with pleasure, with gratification unlike any other.

She rocked and rocked as the waves worked their way through her body and he stayed with her, his touch softening, his kisses travelling up her front until he reached her lips. 'We can take this to bed.'

'No,' she said into his eyes. 'I want you here.'

His body taut with need, his smile twitched. 'Now?'

She slid her palm between their bodies in answer and guided him home. He had to fight to keep his head from rolling back, fight to keep his eyes open as he moved within her, unwilling to break the connection she had forged.

There was no holding back. No worrying about birth control. No layer of protection between them. Physically or mentally. The reminder that she was already pregnant with his child a primal force within and intensifying it all.

He was done for...broken for ever...hers for ever...and he cursed.

Desperate to break the spell. Desperate to push back the declaration that wanted to erupt. Words that she would never want to hear but his heart wanted to declare them anyway.

'That's it, baby, let go for me.'

All for me...and only me.

The walls around his heart were no more, but he didn't stop. Couldn't stop.

Her nails bit into his shoulders as she called his name over and over, and as she found her release, he found his. He felt so connected to her that, in that one blissful moment as he gazed into her glassy greys, he could almost believe they were one—in mind and spirit, heart and soul, in love.

Almost.

'I'm surprised you came tonight.'

Leon shot him a look across the kitchen as he opened the bottle of red Brendan and his date had brought to dinner. In the distance, the chatter of the women could be heard over the festive music playing on the sound system.

'Hannah was very insistent.'

'Well, it's her birthday next week. How could you not, right?'

Brendan refused to rise to the obvious note in his tone. 'Indeed.'

'Besides, we've only seen you once since my thirtieth last year, and she's not stupid. She knows something's up.'

Okay, so he hadn't been going to rise to it, but it seemed Leon was determined to go there...

'You could always tell her the truth.'

Leon gave a laugh that was all the more chilling for the fact it was so easy. 'Tell her that I stole

*your client out from under you? Yeah, sure, that'll
go down so well.'*

*Brendan shrugged. 'I couldn't care less, Leon.
You did what you felt you had to.'*

*And it had exposed his friend for the man he
truly was—desperate, power-hungry and deeply
insecure.*

*'It wasn't like you needed them, Brendan. You
were set to make partner long before I did, thanks
to your name alone. The legal warrior seeking
justice for the Hart family... What firm could resist that?'*

*Brendan clenched his jaw, fending off the pain
of the past. 'I said I don't care, Leon.'*

*'Only you do. Else there wouldn't be this awk-
wardness between us now.'*

*And what could he say to that? Other than,
'You're right.'*

*'Do you know what it's like to constantly be
outshone by your best friend and your wife?'*

*Leon's blue eyes raked over him, the hint of re-
gret and something unidentifiable residing there.*

*'Okay, ex–best friend. No, of course you don't.
How could you possibly?'*

*Brendan sighed. 'Just leave it, okay? Hannah
wants a nice evening...let's give her one.'*

*Now his laugh was cold. 'Of course. Hannah.
It's always about Hannah...the glue that keeps
us together...'*

'I don't want her upset by this.'

'No, you don't ever want her upset by anything. It really must bust your gut every day that I—'

'Leon, don't.'

'Leon? Brendan?'

Hannah's voice cut through the heat of the room, soft, wary.

'Is everything okay?'

He spun to face her. What had she heard? How had he not sensed her come up behind him? Normally he was attuned to her every step...

'Everything's fine, honey,' Leon murmured, saccharine sweet. 'We just need to invest in a better bottle-opener.'

He carried the bottle out, leaving Hannah facing Brendan, her eyes probing.

'Are things fine?' she asked.

Hardly, he wanted to choke out. I'm dating a woman your exact opposite, in the hope that I can eradicate you from my heart, and you're married to a man who doesn't deserve yours.

Aloud, he said, 'How can they not be fine, Han? It's Christmas! The season of peace and goodwill to all men...'

Even those men who didn't deserve it but enjoyed it anyway because of the women in their lives...

CHAPTER FIFTEEN

'WOW,' SHE MURMURED against his chest. 'So that just happened...'

He pressed a kiss to her hair. 'It did.'

She shifted against him, her body suddenly bemoaning the hard surface beneath her, and he tensed.

'Are you okay? Did I hurt you?'

He was already brushing her hair back from her cheeks, tilting her head back to search her eyes. His genuine concern a never-ending threat to her carefully controlled life.

His concern? Why don't you focus on the intense connection and the earth-shattering orgasm he just gave you, twice over, then work out the real threat?

But then it was all part of the same package— the considerate, panty-melting, heart-tugging, alpha package that was Brendan Hart.

'Hannah?'

'*Hurt* me?' she blurted, forcing herself to calm, forcing her tone to be as incredulous as she felt in the face of his question. How could he think he'd hurt her physically when he'd just given her the best sex of her life…on a kitchen counter too. 'I'm pregnant, Brendan, not broken…unless you count having an abnormally high sex drive courtesy of said pregnancy.'

His eyes sparkled, the post-orgasm glow in his cheeks lending him a boyish charm—he appeared younger, happier and more heart-tugging than ever. 'That sounds like a perk to me.'

'Not when it drives you to distraction, it isn't.'

'Is that what I've been doing, driving you to distraction?'

She could see his ego preening beneath the surface and she gave a soft laugh, lowered her lashes. 'I reserve the right to remain silent.'

'Spoilsport.'

Because how could she possibly tell him that she craved him? Day and night. That it wasn't simply an itch that needed scratching, it was a permanent rash.

'I hadn't read about the sex-drive thing.'

'Now that does surprise me, but, I assure you, it's one hundred per cent true. Horny Pregnant Lady can attest to it.'

He chuckled low in his throat.

'It isn't funny.'

'It is kind of funny.'

She shoved him, though she wasn't going anywhere, they were still locked together, her legs hooked around him. 'I'd like to see how you cope with thinking about sex twenty-four-seven.'

'Well, I am a man…'

She laughed. 'I'd noticed.'

'And I guess that makes me a handy solution too?'

She felt her cheeks burn. 'Are you asking whether I used you to scratch an itch?'

'I'm not sure I like that particular term, but…'

She shook her head but sobered with her thoughts as honest as they were…

'Hannah?'

'All jokes aside, Brendan, I don't know what's going on. I'm attuned to you in every way. Whether we're at work, in the car, the midwife's, here…my body knows you're there and it—it craves you.'

His eyes glimmered; his jaw pulsed. 'You crave me?'

'I know I shouldn't. I know we're friends. Just friends, but I don't know. Maybe it's because I have your baby growing inside me, an unbreakable bond. Maybe it's the night we shared which slips into my dreams or interrupts my thoughts when I'm supposed to be working and teases me to distraction. Or maybe it's just you, something about you…' And Lord she was rambling, but she couldn't seem to stop. The honesty and outpouring so refreshing. 'All I know is that I want you and only you, and I'm sorry. I never should have jumped you, like that, like this. I just—I wasn't thinking.'

'Why are you apologising?'

'Because I've muddied our relationship. It's already complicated enough without adding sex into the equation.'

'I hate to tell you this, but that ship sailed over two months ago.'

'You know what I mean.'

'I do, but I still don't see the problem. You want me, and, in case it's escaped your notice, I want you too. Why can't we enjoy this for as long as we want it?'

'You're serious?'

'We're already pregnant, Han…'

'How much worse can it get? Is that what you're saying?'

'No, not at all.'

'You're right though. We hardly planned this and for two people who meticulously plan everything in their lives, work or otherwise, this situation is already messed up enough.'

'We can't change what's done.'

'No, but we don't have to make it any worse either.'

'I think you're overthinking it.'

'And I think you're not thinking enough.'

'Fine, Ice. Let's agree that this was a mistake and move on.'

He went to shift away and the sudden chill through her veins had her clutching him back, nothing to do with the use of her nickname and everything to do with the loss of him. 'No. I don't want that either.'

'Then what do you want? Because right now, you're—'

She cut his words off with a kiss. Hot and urgent and driven by her panic, because when she kissed him the world righted itself and her heart raced, not with panic, but with passion. And that was so much easier to deal with than the issues beneath the surface.

'Okay—' he broke away first, his ragged breath both thrilling and reassuring '—so I don't know what that kiss meant, but I think I need to get you off this counter and feed you some dinner before I take you to bed and ravish you instead.'

'Now who's the spoilsport?'

CHAPTER SIXTEEN

BRENDAN CHECKED HIS WATCH. Almost midnight and still he couldn't sleep.

Curled into his side, Hannah gently snored, her presence as warming as it was unsettling, and he couldn't lie about the cause of his insomnia. It had plagued him for days. Ever since they'd crossed the line and started sleeping together, and he didn't just mean the sex. Which was great. Out-of-this-world great. He meant actually *sleeping* together. In his room that he'd originally given up for her and had swiftly become theirs.

Had he been too rash to suggest it? Yes.

Did he regret it? No.

Because this time with her was precious and very much borrowed. Unless he could find a way to make it permanent. To let this arrangement slip seamlessly into their new life with their child. To live together as a family.

They might not have had an orthodox beginning but that didn't mean they couldn't end up in a normal relationship. That he couldn't have the woman he'd been in love with for as long as he could remember.

And now he had to make a choice, he could be honest with her about his feelings and risk her running. Or he could keep quiet and they could carry on as they were and he would live each day fearing the moment she brought it to an end.

Or worse, met someone else.

She stirred beside him and he realised he was gripping her tight, his tension and desperation overflowing into his hold. It was no use. He couldn't lie there staring at the ceiling wishing sleep would come, wishing he could have all that he desired, all that he almost had...

Carefully, he slid out from underneath her, tugged on his lounge pants, took up his phone and left the room, closing the door quietly behind him. He headed to the living area, the grand piano in the corner beckoning him over. He felt rusty, his fingers tight. How long had it been since he'd played?

Before Hannah it had been work getting in the way and since Hannah it had been this. Their mess, as she'd so aptly put it. He slid onto the stool, placed his phone on the top and lifted the key cover, flexed his fingers and closed his eyes, let age-old intuition take over. He played softly, the tune heavy with his mood, the tempo undulating with it too. He lost sight of where he was, why he was there, let everything around him and the chaos within him fall away...

'Can't sleep?'

He missed a note, his head snapping around to find Hannah a few feet away, a rose-coloured slip skimming her curves in all the right places. His heart and body warmed as his brain cautioned him to go steady.

'Sorry…' He turned in his seat, reached out for her, the move automatic and born of the fragile intimacy that had grown between them. 'Did I wake you?'

She slipped into his arms, placed her phone onto the piano top beside his as she leaned back against his chest. 'Not really. I stirred when you left and saw a message from Jessie that I'd missed earlier. I couldn't settle after I read it and then I heard the piano and wanted to come and listen. I haven't heard you play in a long time.'

He kissed the dip in her shoulder. 'I haven't played in a long time.'

'You wouldn't know it…' She tilted her head to his. 'You're very talented.'

He chuckled low in his throat. 'And when you say it like that, I feel like you're referring to more than just my skills at the piano.'

She laughed softly. 'No comment.'

He treated her to a playful nip of his teeth and she wriggled in closer, her nipples pebbling beneath her slip and brushing against his arm. He could easily continue down this path, kiss and caress her until whatever Jessie had said left her mind, but there'd been enough avoidance already.

'What did Jessie say to worry you?'

'Nothing. Nothing different anyway, I just—
I get the impression she's getting herself in deep
and I'm worried, Brendan. Really worried. I sent
her there. It'll be my fault if he breaks her heart
and—'

'Hey… Hey, shh…' He turned her into him.
'You've got to stop doing this. I know you feel responsible for her but you're not. You love her, she's
your sister, but she's not your responsibility. You
have a child to worry about now, your health too.'

'And I'm worried I've been so distracted by our
child that I've neglected her.'

'You haven't neglected her. You've taken a back
seat just as she requested.'

'And look where that's got me. According to
your villa staff, they're inseparable.'

Worry creased up her brow, the dark shadows
beneath her eyes tugging at his heartstrings. 'You
can't let yourself get worked up like this. It won't
be doing you or the baby any good.'

'That's easier said than done.'

'Right…' He took up his phone, determined
to do more.

'What are you doing?'

'Messaging Joel.'

He tapped out a message, one he probably
should have sent sooner but he'd put his faith in
his friend, maybe too much faith…

She picked up her phone, started typing her own message.

They finished together, and she placed her phone back on the piano.

'What did you say?' he asked.

'I told her I was happy that she was happy but warned her to keep in mind, a fling is a fling, she won't change him. I'm hoping the happy bit will take the sting out of the rest…'

He nodded, projecting none of his inner turmoil. Was that what they were too, a fling? Was that her way of warning Jessie and himself in the same breath? A timely reminder that he couldn't change her either and her heart would always be out of reach.

'What about you?'

Trying to ignore the sinking weight in his gut, he showed her the phone.

'Oh…'

'Oh?'

'That's quite…'

'Blunt?'

'Yes.'

'I thought you wanted me to be blunt.'

'Yes, but… I don't know. That's quite the ultimatum.'

'I know.'

'But he's your best friend?'

'I know that too.'

She stared back at him, eyes wide.

'Do you want me to take it back?'

She hesitated, then, 'No...though I don't want to come between the two of you.'

'He did that when he went against my request.'

'But to say that you'll be done with him...'

'If he breaks her heart after everything she's been through then promises must have been made, and in my world you don't break a promise, no matter how torn up you are.'

Whatever she saw in his face had her grey eyes shining.

'Why couldn't more men be like you?'

His heart swelled. His head screamed. *It doesn't mean she loves you!*

'Just because Leon was—'

'No, not just Leon, my father too. You're a diamond in the rough, Brendan.'

'If you say so...' He was trying to downplay it; he *needed* to downplay it.

'But I played my part in the breakdown of my marriage. I may have been faithful for as long as we were together, but I know Leon's right on some level. I didn't give him what he needed. I didn't love him like he craved.'

'He should have left you first though, Han. What he did was wrong, no matter which way you look at it.'

'It doesn't matter any more. Soon the paperwork will be done with and I'll be free of that mistake. As for Jessie, I'll be happy when I see her for myself and can come clean about everything. Keeping it from her has only made me feel worse, you were right about that.'

'I take it you still want to fly out and see her before she leaves.'

'Please.'

'Of course, but until then, you need to focus on you and our baby.'

The lines deepened around her eyes, his words having the opposite effect to what he intended.

'I know.' She gave him a small smile. 'Can I ask you something?'

'Of course.'

'What were you were playing when I came in?'

'Something and nothing.'

'It was your own piece?'

'I wouldn't call it a piece, more of a feeling...'

'Playing out your mood?'

'Basically.'

'And what were you feeling to play something so melancholic?'

The hairs on his neck rose, the warning in his brain loud and clear. *You can't tell her the truth.*

Because that would mean telling her that he feared a future where she was always on the periphery rather than at the heart of it. He wanted his life to revolve around her, them, their child. He didn't want to lead a separate life, coming together for the sake of their child and only then.

'Brendan?'

'I'd prefer to call it thoughtful.'

Her lips twitched. 'About?'

'The future. Where we'll live, *how* we'll live…'

Her lashes fluttered and she looked away from him. 'You mean custody arrangements?'

He didn't answer, he didn't need to.

'It's been on my mind a lot too. I don't want to be apart from my child.'

'I assume you'll take mat leave…'

'Of course, but I mean after that.'

'When you go back to work?'

She nodded.

'I told you, I'll take a step back from the firm, pick up most of the childcare.'

She tensed but said nothing.

'What's wrong?'

Nothing.

'Hannah?'

'I don't want my child living apart from me.'

It came out in a rush, confirmation of a future he didn't want either, but what was the alternative?

'You want to continue working full-time, though?'

'I want to find some balance, whether that's full-time or four days a week. I just know I want us to live under the same roof.'

'And what about me? Where do I fit in this plan?' He regretted it as soon as it was out, regretted it all the more as she got to her feet and walked up to the glass, her arms wrapped around her middle. 'Maybe now isn't the best time for this discussion.'

But when would be…? They couldn't avoid it for ever, as much as she might want to.

'I'm not sure there'll ever be a best time, as you put it.'

She shook her head, gave a harsh laugh. 'You don't want me stressed out but you're happy to go head-to-head on custody arrangements with a baby that isn't even born yet?'

No, he wasn't happy about it. He wasn't happy about anything because he couldn't look to the future when it meant accepting their separation and the child caught in the middle. He couldn't look to the future and not want a plan in place. A plan that cemented them together.

A plan that…that…

'I'm not even three months gone yet, Brendan, anything could happen.'

'Don't say that.'

'You said it.'

'And I told you no more. I want to look to the future with you and our baby firmly in it, Hannah. I want us to be able to make plans and look forward to it, rather than fear it.'

'And that means talking about custody, right now?'

'It means talking about what we want that future to look like, yes.'

She turned to eye him head-on. 'And just how does that future look to you?'

He stood and closed the distance between them, his heart galloping at a million miles an hour, his head racing ahead with a plan that made so much sense. So much sense and yet the little voice at the back of his mind was telling him to kill off the idea before it took hold, but...

'You really want to know?'

She wet her lips. 'Yes.'

'There's one solution to all our worries, one that makes perfect sense...'

Her eyes narrowed, her head tilting to one side. 'Is that so?'

'Marry me, Hannah.'

'You can't be serious.' Butterflies took off inside her chest as she blinked up at him. 'I can't marry you.'

'Why not?'

'Because I'm still married, for one.'

'I'm not suggesting we go out tomorrow and do it.'

'Brendan, come on...'

'What, Hannah?'

He couldn't be serious. This was Brendan. Wonderful, caring, sweet and clever, deliciously sexy Brendan. He could have any woman he wanted. He deserved someone who could love him freely, without restraint, without fear. She couldn't be her mother, led by her heart. She couldn't be her father, violent with it. Just as she had failed Leon, she would only fail Brendan too. So, no, absolutely not. She couldn't marry him.

'You're not thinking straight.'

'I've never been more rational or clear of thought.'

'But it's crazy.' She paced away, unable to meet the intensity in his gaze without giving fuel to the fire that was her heart and the impossible sense that all he was offering was everything…if only she'd open herself up to it.

'No more crazy than you being pregnant with my child.'

'That was an accident,' she threw back at him, her feet rooted into the floor as she stood her ground. 'You're talking about purposefully making a mistake.'

'Why are you so convinced it would be a mistake?' There was something about the look in his eye that sent a shiver down her spine. His face an impassable mask. 'You married Leon for a lot less than what we have.'

'Don't bring Leon into this.'

'Why not? Scared it'll make you see how wrong he was and how right this is?'

'*Right?* In what way can this be right?'

'You can't deny we have chemistry, we work well in the bedroom, and we work well out of it. We know each other. We can share caseloads as well as parental responsibility. We can make a marriage work for us and we can make a happy home for our child.'

'Come on, Brendan, getting married for the sake of a child, it's bad enough when people use a baby to try and heal their relationship. You want ours to create one.'

'Are you saying what we have isn't a relationship?'

'We're having sex, Brendan. Great sex, but it's still just sex.'

'And nothing more?'

'Don't look at me like that. You knew what this was when we started it.' She was off again, unable to stay still, her bare feet padding across the wooden floor, her eyes on anything but him. 'I knew we never should have crossed the line. I knew we were muddying the waters. I knew—I knew—'

'Stop running away, Han, and look at me!' His hand closed around her elbow, his sudden touch sending sparks through her middle while her panicked heart had her leaping away.

'What?' she blurted.

'Neither of us want to be without our child, neither of us want to be an absentee parent. If we're together under one roof, a family, we both get what we want, and our child has the best of both of us. We can move to my place in the country, make it a family home again. It's a little further out but we can make it work and you can have all the space that you need.'

'Hart Mansion? But you haven't been there in years.'

'Because the bad memories took out the good. This would be a chance to make new memories, happy ones, fill the walls with laughter again.'

'Now I know you're dreaming.'

'There's nothing to stop us making that dream a reality, Han. Just think about it. You know it makes sense.'

She was shaking her head. 'I can't.'

'Why?'

'Because you shouldn't marry me because it's convenient.'

'And you shouldn't have married Leon because you felt he was a safe bet.'

'I didn't.'

'No? Then tell me why you did, because from where I'm standing you never loved him.'

'I never felt out of control with him.'

'And you do with me?'

'Yes—hell, yes!'

He yanked her to his chest, kissed her with feverish intent, his sweet invasion shooting fire to her toes as she sank against him.

'People go their whole lives without this,' he rasped against her lips, as breathless and ragged as she felt. 'Do you really want to spend the rest of yours without it?'

'Lust has an expiry date, Brendan.'

He stared down into her eyes, his lips parting to say something, but the flicker in his eyes told her he'd chosen another path. 'I can make you feel safe, Han, I swear it.'

'No—no, you can't.' She shook her head as she pressed away from him, unable to be this close to him without losing sight of what was right. 'You make me feel all kinds of vulnerable, and I can't go there. I can't. My father may have been an alcoholic, but he claimed love was the poison that had him striking out, and it broke my mother, who was forever chasing it. What if my father's right? What if love is like a poison to my family? I won't be like them, Brendan. I won't.'

'Love didn't make your parents that way, Han. They did. And just because they behaved one way, it doesn't follow that you will be the same. You're your own woman, you of all people should know that.'

'My own woman when I'm not even divorced and I'm already pregnant to another man.' She gave a derisive laugh as her stomach turned over. 'Now you want to add a marriage into the mix… we're going to be a laughing stock as it is.'

'Do you really care what people think?'

'You *know* I care. It's bad enough that news of Leon's affair has been spread about. I can just imagine how this is going to go down.'

'You can't hide the fact that you're pregnant, we've already—'

'*No*, but I don't need to hand them more ammunition with another marriage. I can hear the stories now—she didn't hang around long, did she? So afraid to be on her own she got herself pregnant and backed poor sweet Brendan into a corner, quite the catch, he really doesn't deserve to be landed with her, of all people. The woman has no heart, no decency!'

'Or it goes the other way...'

'Which is?'

He surprised her by sweeping the back of his hand across her cheek, gentle, soothing, his eyes not losing their blazing intensity, only deepening. 'That they think we're desperately in love.'

She froze. He couldn't—he wasn't—*was* he?

His hand fell away, his eyes hardening at whatever he read in hers. 'Don't look so pale, Hannah. It's just the "L" word and, believe you me, if we paint the picture, they'll lap it up. No one will dare argue with it.'

'You want us to pretend to be in love?'

Why was the idea killing her so much? Why did his proposal of convenience sting so much? Why did she feel as if she were dying on the inside? Her heart shrivelling up, worn and cold.

'Forget I said anything.' He dropped back, freeing her from his grasp and making her feel his loss a thousand times over. 'Your face says it all.'

She shook her head. How could she make him see? How could she make him understand when she didn't understand it herself?

'I'll give you some space. I can see you don't need me here right now.'

The truth was she did need him—physically, mentally, emotionally—and admitting it was terrifying. Admitting what it meant, all the more so.

'Where are you going?'

Her voice was so quiet, so strained and he didn't pause. Had he not heard her? She chased after him, her heart taking a jolt. *Brendan!'*

He turned on his heel, his expression like steel, and she dropped back. 'Please, don't go like this.'

His lashes flickered, the slightest softening in his gaze. 'I have to.'

She wet her lips. 'This is your home. If anyone is to leave…'

'No.' He was severe. Hard. 'You stay. Charles will check on you until I return. After that we'll figure out some arrangement to make sure you're okay. You and the baby.'

Something about the way he said the last made her shiver, his meaning hitting home—some arrangement where they were no longer living together.

She nodded. His jaw pulsed, his eyes raked over her face, the burn of so much residing there, and then he was gone, quicker than she could blink… a chilling coldness left in his wake.

You should be happy, grateful, relieved.
So why did it feel as though the bottom had fallen out of her world…?

CHAPTER SEVENTEEN

'*Lust has an expiry date, Brendan.*'
Love doesn't, Hannah.

The response revolved around his mind as though he'd said it aloud, his eyes locked on the blood seeping from her face as she'd gazed at him in horror.

Only he hadn't said it aloud. It was his dream torturing him, his mind in that weird space between awake and asleep. Reality mixing with fantasy—though no fantasy that he'd ever want to live through.

'Brendan, you up? Brendan!'

An incessant knocking accompanied the shout and he shot forward, an almighty pain behind his eyes as he gripped his head.

'Brendan!'

Where the hell was he? He planted his feet on the ground, hunched forward and scanned the room… The wall lined with books, the desk complete with banker's lamp and empty whisky bottle, two tumblers beside it, the Chesterfield armchair and the sofa beneath him. The tartan throw over his thighs. Simon's.

'Brendan?' The door opened and the man himself peered around it.

'What time is it?' His mouth felt woolly, his voice thick.

'Just gone six. I wouldn't have woken you but it's Joel. He says it's urgent.'

'Joel?' He grimaced as adrenaline shot through him. There was only one reason Joel would ring so early… 'Why didn't he just call me?'

Simon entered the room and handed him his phone. It had to be one in the morning in Mustique and his gut rolled as he recalled the last message he'd sent… Had that triggered the call, or had something happened? Something bad?

'He did, your phone isn't connecting.'

Brendan cursed, tugged his jacket off the back of the sofa and pulled out his phone—dead.

'Here, give it to me. I'll get it on charge…you ring Joel back.'

'Any idea what's wrong?'

'Not a clue, but I suggest you ring him and then hit the shower. You look rough.'

He was about to tell Simon he had a nerve telling him that, but the guy was far too fresh in the face. 'And you look like you didn't share the best part of a whisky bottle with me…'

'The benefit of youth, my friend.'

'Two years younger, Simon. Two years.' He snatched the phone from him, his mind immediately shifting gears as the feeling of dread spread through his system.

He dialled Joel and the ringing tone cut off abruptly with his friend's voice. 'Simon?'

'It's me, Brendan.'

'Thank God…'

Knees to her chest, Hannah stared at her phone on the sofa before her, willing it to ring.

The sun was on the rise, casting squares of amber across the room, its warmth doing nothing to ease the empty chill inside. She'd given up on sleep hours ago, taking to the living area in the hope that Brendan would return. He hadn't.

She hadn't heard from Charles either, which begged the question, just how did he intend the man to check on her?

Were there cameras in this room? Was the man watching her right now as she fretted? Sleep-starved and irrational with it. Because the more she thought on it, the more she realised she was falling in love with Brendan, *was* in love with Brendan, and it was everything she'd fought so hard against her entire life.

Her fingers trembled as she smoothed her hair back into its tie, a nervous move she had repeated over and over as she waited and waited. Anything to stop herself from sending him another message and hounding him. One was enough. One to ask when he would be back and she'd got nothing.

She tapped the screen to check the time. Almost seven. It was too early to ring him, but—

The sound of the lift arriving sent her heart into a spin and she twisted in her seat. The sight of him stepping into the room sent a woosh of delight charging through her. Delight and trepidation, an unsettling mix.

'Brendan...' She shoved herself to standing, strode forward and then stopped herself. He didn't want her near him, that much was obvious. He couldn't even look at her. As for him, he looked like hell.

She wrapped her arms around herself, hugging the sweater she was wearing—*his* sweater—but at least he was back, at least they could now talk. 'I'm so glad you're—'

'My car is waiting to take us to your place. You need to pack a suitcase...'

Her heart slowed, the warm elation she'd felt at his return dimming with every word. He wanted her out already, there was to be no conversation, no nothing.

Can you blame him?

'Okay...if that's what you want, I'll get it done now.'

She headed for the bedroom. 'No, Hannah, that's not what I mean. You need to...' He stopped, his eyes taking her in for the first time. 'Is that my sweater?'

She looked down at the soft navy fabric, heat

creeping into her cheeks. How could she tell him she'd found comfort in his scent, in its familiar warmth, while he'd been gone?

'I'm sorry. I hope you don't mind. I just… I was cold.'

His eyes lifted to hers and she lost the ability to breathe, the fire in his depths branding her so completely. She was his. She felt it to her core, her body drifting towards him, and then the shutter fell. His expression closing off. Whatever she'd spied in his gaze was gone and she felt exposed, wounded, raw.

'I'm sorry,' she repeated, moving again before the ache inside immobilised her completely. 'I'll make sure I put it back where I found it.'

'You don't understand, Hannah. We're leaving for Mustique today.'

She froze. 'What's happened?'

'You need to get dressed and then I'm taking you to your place so you can pack. You'll need cooler clothing.'

'That's not what I asked.' She turned back to him, her eyes narrowing on the dark shadows beneath his eyes, the deep grooves either side of his mouth, the thickening five-o'clock shadow and his hair in disarray. She'd assumed she was the cause, but now… 'We weren't due to leave until next weekend, so I repeat, what's happened?'

'I'll explain on the way.'

'Brendan? Is Jessie okay?'

'We need to move, Hannah. If we don't get going soon, we won't make it before nightfall, and we'll be stuck on Saint Vincent until morning.'

'Why the sudden urgency?'

He raked a hand through his hair, blew out a breath.

'Brendan—' her heart was pulsing wildly in her throat '—if you don't want me to stress out even further, you need to tell me.'

'Joel called.'

She pressed a hand to her throat as last night's dinner threatened to return. 'And?'

'It's as you feared.'

She shook her head, her words tripping over themselves. 'She's in love with him?'

He didn't answer. He didn't need to. 'And Joel? I take it the feeling's not mutual.'

Again, nothing.

'Why did he ring you, then? To tell you in person that he'd broken his promise, to beg you to forgive him for messing up, for screwing around with my sister when you explicitly told him not to?'

She was burning up, bile singeing the back of her throat.

'Take a breath, Hannah. This isn't good for you or—'

'Don't you presume to tell me what's good for me, Brendan.' She strode forward, poked his chest, her anger overflowing with her sadness, her worry. 'You're the one who took off last night and left me stirring, unable to sleep, unable to quit worrying, unable to—to— God, you men are all the same and us women are fools to let you get the better of us.'

He didn't even flinch, just took her battery of abuse as though he deserved it when, in actual fact, he'd tried to do right by her, by their baby, he'd tried to marry her, for Pete's sake, and here she was taking it all out on him.

But this was Jessie. Her little sister, Jessie. And if anyone was to blame, it was her for sending Jessie there.

'Please, go get ready, Han. I want to be gone in five.'

'No.' She shook her head. 'No. I need to speak to her...'

She was already lifting her phone and he stopped her, his hand firm on hers.

'I know you do, but it's the middle of the night out there and you don't want to do this over the phone. The sooner we get airborne, the sooner you can see her and put your mind at rest.'

'What about work?'

'I've taken care of it.'

She wanted to argue with him, but how could she when she knew he was right? Knew he was right and knew that he was doing this for her. For her and for Jessie.

No matter that Joel was his friend, that she'd outright rejected his offer of marriage and pushed him away, he was still trying to help her. And she didn't deserve it. No more than she deserved him, the one man she had come to love against the odds but didn't trust herself to keep.

CHAPTER EIGHTEEN

SIXTEEN HOURS LATER, they were being thrown around in the back of the Jeep. But he couldn't blame Paolo, his driver, or the uneven terrain for the sickness in his gut.

No, that was all down to the woman beside him and the guy in the passenger seat.

Joel was a hot mess. Beneath his tan, he looked pale, the sheen of sweat across his brow persisting in spite of the air conditioning. All because Jessie had told him that she loved him, that she wanted a future with him…and he'd choked.

Choked and called Brendan—desperate, guilt-stricken, a mess—and Brendan had done the one thing he knew he could do, he'd brought their flight forward. Seeing to it that Jessie would have Hannah in the aftermath of their breakup and Joel would be free to leave. Though being free to leave and being free of his own feelings for the woman were not one and the same and Brendan wondered whether his friend would realise it any time soon.

As for Hannah, if Joel was pale, she was positively ghostlike. Her subtle make-up doing nothing to hide her pallor or the shadows that spread like bruises beneath her eyes. Several times he'd caught her pressing her fingers to her mouth, a thin layer of perspiration breaking across her upper lip, her simple slip of a dress concealing any show of her pregnancy. She looked too thin, too drawn, too broken, and it was tearing him apart.

But Hannah, being Hannah, had held her head high when he'd introduced her to Joel, a brusque nod had been his lot. No verbal abuse, just quiet disregard.

Dammit, Joel.

Why couldn't his friend have toed the line for once in his life?

No, that wasn't fair. The man had spent his life toeing the line up until the day he'd lost his wife. These last two years had been payback to a life that had ruined him. And here they were at loggerheads because he'd deigned to hurt the one woman he'd been told to leave well alone.

If only things could be different. If only Joel weren't so messed up. If only Jessie had been the one to help him…to change him.

If only Brendan could be the one to change Hannah, too, but then life was never so simple or fair.

Fifteen years of loving Hannah from afar should have taught him that.

He took her in now, sitting as far away from him as she could manage, legs and body angled towards the window, eyes fixated on the back of Joel's head as if she could murder him with her mind.

Would it be like this if he hadn't done the unthinkable and proposed? Pushing for what he wanted. What he saw to be the perfect solution—to her worries and his own deepest desire.

He might as well have declared his undying love for her and been done with it because the way she looked at him now, the way she avoided his eye and the slightest touch, it couldn't be any worse.

The Jeep jerked to a stop outside the villa and Joel was already moving, throwing off his seat belt without a backward glance. 'Just give me a minute.'

It wasn't a request. He raced off, slamming the door shut behind him, and Hannah looked to Brendan.

'Are you okay?' Even as he asked it the sheen over her skin thickened and she licked her lips. He didn't need an answer.

'I think I'm going to be sick.'

'I'll get you inside.'

He started to move. Joel would have to have his time later, but as he thought it he saw Jessie emerge from the undergrowth and Hannah put her hand on his arm. 'Hang on.'

Hannah's voice was strained but her gaze was sharp. Whatever she saw in Jessie's face gave her reason to pause and as he took in the redhead's face, so similar to and yet so different from her sister's, he could see why. The woman's smile was so full of love it was impossible not to pause, to take it in, and as she and Joel came together the warmth of their connection radiated out.

The man was a fool, Brendan decided, an absolute fool to have that and turn it away.

'Shall I get the cases out, boss?' Paolo caught his attention and he nodded, his gaze returning to the couple now talking as Paolo stepped out.

It wasn't going well. Jessie's smile morphed into confusion as Joel hurried forward, took her hand. He started to pull her away and Hannah tensed beside Brendan. 'Where does he think he's going?'

She pressed the back of her hand to her lips, the exclamation taking it out of her.

'We're getting you inside.' He threw open his door, his only thought to ease Hannah's concern and get her to the bathroom. 'That's enough, Joel!'

'I asked you to wait, Brendan!' his panicked friend threw back at him, his blue eyes wide as Jessie spun to face him too.

'Brendan?' she whispered, her confused frown speaking volumes.

'We've waited too long as it is…' He should have taken Hannah straight inside, told Joel to hang back, not the other way around. 'Hannah needs to use the bathroom.'

'Hannah?' Jessie's eyes snapped to the car as her sister stepped out beside him. 'Sis! What on earth are you—?' She was upon them in a second, her arms wrapped around her sister, squeezing tight. For a horrible second, he thought Hannah might lose her dinner right there.

'Are you finally taking a holiday and crashing mine?'

Hannah gave a laugh, but it was as high and as awkward as her sister sounded, her arms around Jessie stiff as she leaned back to scan her face. 'Are you okay?'

'How many times do I have to tell you, I'm fine?' Jessie pressed her further away to eye her top to toe and Brendan could see the concern in her gaze before she even said, 'You don't look so hot though.'

Hannah's eyes flitted to his and he felt his heart pulse. 'I really do need the toilet.'

'Sure, sure,' Jessie rushed out over any response he could have given, 'I'll show you the—'

'Brendan can show her,' Joel interjected. 'We need to talk.'

Joel met his eye, silently pleading for the time alone to explain. To try and ease some of the damage he had done… There was something else there, too. Something not so very different from what he saw in Jessie's gaze. Did his friend really think his heart had remained untouched? Was he really that blind to it?

He gave him a nod, his hand lowering to Hannah's back as he gently ushered her towards the house, wishing he could take away her sickness, wishing he could wake Joel up to what he could have if he opened up his heart again…

'Mr Hart, Miss Rose, I trust you had a good journey.' His butler, Anton, appeared as they entered, behind him his housekeeper, June, carried a tray with fresh juice, but he could feel the rising tension in Hannah's spine. 'Would you care for some refreshment?'

Hannah gave them a weak smile.

'Just give us a moment, Anton.' He led her towards the nearest bathroom, calling back to Anton. 'If you can ensure Joel's bags are loaded into the Jeep, that would be great.'

'Certainly.'

'Thank you,' Hannah murmured softly.

'For what?'

'For bringing me.'

She shouldn't be thanking him. This whole mess was his fault. It had happened on his watch, under his roof…

She closed the door on him and he stood there, helpless and worthless, wanting to lay his heart on the line but knowing he couldn't. To tell Hannah he loved her only to have her reject that love… there could be no coming back from that. So he kept his lips sealed and concentrated on the one thing he could fix—Jessie and Joel.

Whether that meant kicking his friend's arse to make him realise what was right in front of his nose or seeing him gone so that Jessie could heal, he would play his part.

Protector to Hannah and those she loved, even if he could never be included in that precious circle.

Hannah splashed cool water on her face, dabbed it dry and stared at herself in the mirror. Only, it didn't feel as if she were looking at herself.

The drawn expression, the shadowed eyes, the hair that had started to escape its tie and the gentle swell to her tummy beneath her summer dress. Indiscernible if you didn't know it existed but everything to her.

Her biggest secret and one that she had kept from Jessie for far too long. That and her broken marriage, which now felt like a distant memory not a huge failing in her present.

And seeing her sister, knowing how much she had kept from her these past few months, was chewing her up inside.

As for Brendan, the man had done so much for her, so much for her sister too, gifting her a place on this scale...

She'd scarce paid attention to the house as they'd pulled up, other than a vague awareness of its sheer size and the way the natural grey stone and teak blended into its tropical surroundings, the large glass windows reflecting it all back at you. Inside it was the picture of calm too. Dark wooden floors rolling into white walls, colourful wall hangings and exposed beams, woven furniture with plush and inviting cushions, various plants bringing the outside in. Even the air was scented—a soothing mix of jasmine and ylang ylang—and she breathed it in as she tried to quit the tremble in her fingers...in her heart.

It was all so very Brendan. Impressive but subtle with it. Imposing yet sympathetic. And everything to her bruised and battered heart.

One that had swooped when she'd witnessed Jessie's face stepping from the undergrowth, her eyes on Joel and a smile so full of her love for him. To know that Joel too was suffering—she hadn't been blind to his genuine distress or the love she was convinced existed for him to be in such pain. It had reminded her too much of herself...

Running from the one thing that her heart so keenly wanted, the gulf between her and the man who owned this piece of paradise growing by the hour, not the day.

She felt as though she were on a treadmill racing towards an ending she didn't want with no hope of changing direction or hopping off.

Her life wasn't her own any more.

Her plans weren't her own.

And her heart...her heart wanted what she'd always refused to give it.

Love.

A knock on the door made her start, Jessie's voice quick to follow. 'Han! You all right?'

She was supposed to be here for Jessie, to support Jessie, instead she was the one hiding away and falling apart while she was it.

'Han!'

She pulled open the door, plastered on a smile but as soon as she set eyes on her sister's concerned face she crumbled. Tears falling, a sob rising up that she couldn't contain.

Get a grip, you're the big sister!

'You need to get a grip, sis.' Jessie's eyes blazed with passion and unshed tears, but her voice was steady as she vocalised Hannah's mental admonishment. 'I'm fine. Honestly, I'm fine.'

Hannah looked to the open doorway, the men's voices carrying on the invading breeze but indiscernible across the distance. Was Brendan telling Joel their news, was it all to come out that day? The baby, his practical proposal, her refusal…

She started to sob all over again. She wanted to take it back. She wanted him to love her as she had come to love him. But not because he had to. Because he wanted to.

And where did that leave them?

Jessie shot her a look. 'Jesus, Han, calm down. Everything's fine, I promise.'

She never cried, not like this, but it was as if a tap had been twisted on and there was no way of stemming the flow. The tears or the pain. 'No, it's not fine, nothing is.'

'So, I fell in love with the wrong guy, again—

it's not the end of the world! I don't need you to sort me out, okay? I'm quite capable of doing that myself.' Jessie's voice escalated with every word, her frustration mounting as she misread her sister's reaction. And Hannah couldn't blame her, she'd been suffocating her with her concern these last few weeks, her whole life even, and now here she was having a breakdown over her own life and the mess she had caused, and Jessie hadn't a clue about any of it.

'I know you're worried about me,' Jessie was saying, 'but this has to stop. I'm a fully grown adult, capable of making my own mistakes and learning from them. I don't need you protecting me all the time, smothering me and mollycoddling me. I don't need—'

'I know you are, Jess.' Hannah shook her head rapidly. 'I'm sorry I've made you feel that way.'

Her sister's frown was sharp, her eyes sharper still. 'You're really starting to worry me, Han. What's going on?'

Hannah shook with another sob and this time she didn't hold back, her body folding in on itself as she hugged her growing bump.

Jessie shot forward, her arms coming round her. 'Hey, hey, it's okay… Shh, honey, whatever it is, I'm sure it's okay…just talk to me.'

Hannah burrowed her head into Jessie's shoulder. 'You really don't need this right now…'

'That's where you're wrong, sis. For the first

time in your life, you need me and I'm here. This is everything I need right now, believe me.'

Jessie's voice was so strong, so reassuring and she was right, for the first time ever, Hannah didn't feel as if she had to be the responsible one, the strong one, the protective one. She let her sister be all that and more. 'I'm pregnant, Jess.'

'Wow, Han, that's—that's *amazing*! Isn't it?'

Hannah threw her head up, looked down into her sister's blue eyes and admitted with all of her heart, 'It's Brendan's.'

Jessie's mouth fell open, her arms going limp around her. 'It's...*whose*?'

'Brendan's.'

'That's what I thought you said.' She fell back a step, shook her head. 'But what about Leon?'

She swallowed and the guilt, the weight of her secret, the love that she couldn't let in, rose to the surface, suffocating her, cutting off her ability to speak.

'I think we should sit down for this...' Jessie was guiding her off and she followed, blind to her surroundings until she was ushered into a deep-back sofa, the sound of water trickling and gentle music a backdrop to her pounding heart. They were surrounded by the outdoors through the glass walls and books on the other. A library. A Jessie haven. 'You'd best start from the beginning, sis.'

And so she did. She poured her heart into her

words, told her of Leon, the affairs, the day that
Brendan came to her over a year ago and the day
she had gone to his almost three months ago. The
resulting baby and the proposal born of convenience.

'I can't believe you're only just telling me this
now, sis. You *should* have told me. You shouldn't
have gone through all this alone.'

'You had so much going on. I didn't want to
add to it.'

'But to keep it from me, to make me think you
and Leon were okay…? I could kill him.'

'It wasn't his fault, not really.'

'So you say, but whatever was going on between you both, it doesn't give him the right to
go looking for that love and affection elsewhere.
It's wrong and he should've been man enough to
have it out with you before it got to that point. He's
as bad as Adam.'

'I won't argue with you there.'

'So, what now?'

'I don't know. I'm so scared. I never thought I'd
be a mother, Jess, and for the first time in my life I
have no plan, no way of knowing if I can do this.'

'You're the strongest woman I know, sis. You
can and will get through this. I don't doubt it for a
second. And from what you're saying, you're not
doing it alone either. You have Brendan.'

'But I don't want Brendan. Not like this.'

'What do you mean?'

'I don't want a marriage of convenience. I've already lived through one and look how that ended.'

'But Brendan isn't Leon.'

'No, he's not, he's really not. But a child isn't a reason to get married.'

'I won't deny that but—'

'And I'm pregnant, Jess. Pregnant! What do I know about being a mother? About loving a child? What if I'm an awful mother? What if I can't love them like I should? I'm incapable of loving someone properly, if Leon is to be believed.'

Jessie shook her head, tears welling in her eyes as she smoothed Hannah's escaped hair back from her face and held her steady to her words. 'You've loved me for my entire life. You brought me up when Mum and Dad were distracted with their own lives. You've been the responsible one. The one cheering me on or disciplining me when I needed it. You protected me. Yes, you've been overbearing, suffocating and a complete nightmare at times, but all because you love me. And when you love someone, you love them with your all, and your child will be no different. I promise you that, Han.'

She stared into her sister's earnest gaze and her heart softened, her pulse slowed...

'She's right.' Brendan's voice came from the doorway and her soothed heart leapt. 'For once in your life, listen to your little sister and trust in what she says.'

'Brendan…?' How long had he been standing there for? How much had he heard?

'I just came to say we're leaving.' He'd never looked more handsome or more forlorn. 'You ladies have the use of this place for as long as you need it. My jet will return you both home when you're ready. Anton will make the arrangements.'

'But…'

Her words trailed off. But what? She could hardly plead with him to stay when he was taking Joel away, giving Jessie some much-needed space.

'We can talk when you get back, put some plans in place.'

The plans that kept them apart and took care of both her and their baby. She wanted to run up to him, throw her arms around his neck, beg him to stay, beg him to take her refusal back. But she couldn't.

He deserved to find love. He deserved that life. Even if she wasn't a part of it, their baby always would be. And that was what mattered most.

She'd find her way again on her own, wouldn't she?

But as she watched him walk away, she couldn't help the feeling that her life was walking away with him.

'Go after him, Han.'

'I can't.'

'Can't or won't?'

'Does it matter which?'

'It does if you love him, like I think you do...'

'How can you possibly...?'

'It's in your face, Han. Every time you mention him or the baby, you have this look about you.'

'The same look you have when you think of Joel?'

Jessie gave her a sad smile. 'Precisely.'

CHAPTER NINETEEN

Two weeks later

'YOU'VE CHANGED THE LOCKS.'

Hannah paused in the outer hallway, her suitcase almost running her feet over. Leon was lounging against the wall beside her front door, his foppish blond hair over one accusatory blue eye.

'You moved out and took a key with you...' Head down, she strode forward. She was exhausted through travel, all she wanted was a bath to try and feel somewhat human again. The sickness was easing, but the needing to pee and sleep was not. And the last thing she needed was a showdown with him, of all people. 'What did you expect me to do?'

'Ask for it back.' He pushed himself straight and held it out to her.

She huffed, shoving her own key into the lock. 'You can throw it.' She unlocked the door and pushed it open. 'Why are you here, Leon?'

'Been somewhere nice?' He gestured to the case as she tugged it over the threshold and he followed close behind.

'Mustique with Jessie. Not that it's any of your business.'

'You finally took some time off, then?'

She bristled. 'Did you come here for something specific or just to pass judgement on my life?'

'Sorry, Han. I didn't come here to argue. Mum asked if I could find the vase Aunt Beth gave us for our wedding, it's a family heirloom apparently…'

'I could have shipped it to you.'

'I wanted to see you too. I wanted to—to see how you were doing…really doing.'

She gave a scoff. 'And you couldn't ask me that in an email or on the phone?'

'I wanted to see you for myself but you're clearly doing great. You look well, really well…a bit of sun suits you.'

His soft sincerity chipped away at her resolve, and she moved before he could say anything more. Tugging off her coat, she headed to the kitchen. 'Well, now you've seen me alive and kicking, you can consider your conscience cleared and go…'

She pulled the vase out of the cupboard beneath the sink and passed it to him. 'Give my love to your mum and close the door on your way out, won't you?'

He turned away and she did the same, his footsteps retreating, the soft click of the door signalling his exit, and she blew out a breath. Grateful that she no longer had an audience, even more grateful that the painful stab of regret no longer existed where Leon was concerned.

No, that was reserved for the man that truly owned her heart, and a fortnight in Mustique with Jessie still hadn't given her any resolution. Tie him into a loveless marriage on his part, have the family life they both wanted for their child, or…or what?

She turned to get a glass for some water and jumped out of her skin. 'Leon!'

'Sorry, Han, I'm not quite finished.'

'You scared the—'

His eyes were pinned at waist level, a deep groove between his brows, and her hand instinctively went to her stomach.

'There's something else I—I need to tell you…' He dragged his eyes up to hers, the very obvious question residing there and she could see him wrestling with it. Telling himself it couldn't be. 'I've asked Christy to marry me as soon as the divorce goes through.'

'You have?' She swallowed, ignoring the way the news pricked at her, brought back her conversation with Brendan, the judgement of others, too. 'You don't hang about, do you?'

'We're in love, Han. It's taken us all this time to find one another and we don't want to waste a second more. We want to start our life, a family…'

His eyes dipped once more and her fingers flexed in their protective grip.

'I didn't want you hearing about it through someone else.'

'That's good of you.' And she softened her tone as his eyes flashed back at her. 'I mean it, Leon. Thank you.' She'd learned of everything else through whispers and till receipts so maybe he was improving, maybe love had made a better man of him. 'I wish you every happiness, Leon.'

He stared at her, the question still blazing along with something else—was that regret?

'I truly am sorry for what happened between us, Hannah. Really, I am. I was just—I was so lost and unhappy and, in truth, I didn't know what I was missing until I met Christy.'

She flinched, not because of him and his new love, but because she felt the same way. She hadn't known what she had been missing until Brendan had shown her another way to feel. Deeply. Unequivocally. Passionately and absolutely. In love.

'I should have ended things between us first and I'm sorry I didn't. I'm sorry I hurt you, Han. I hope that one day you can forgive me.'

Tears pricked out of nowhere and she felt as if she were choking. Choking on her love for Brendan, her regret too...

'Han?' Leon stepped towards her, his panic clear in his widened gaze. Because even at their worst, she hadn't cried on him.

'I'm happy for you, Leon, really.' She backed away. 'But you should go.'

Before she truly did crumble…

He ran a hand through his hair, hesitated on the spot, his eyes flitting to her stomach and back up. 'Okay, Han. Take care of yourself, won't you?'

He was turning away when she yelled, 'Wait!' her heart launching into her throat as she realised she couldn't let him go. Not yet. He might have hurt her, humiliated her, lied to her even, but he'd done the right thing now and she owed him the same. She needed to do the decent thing and come clean, tell him the news before he heard it on the grapevine…

He was frowning at her, patiently waiting, and she took a breath, blurting it out before she could stop herself.

'I'm pregnant.'

His eyes widened. 'I did—I saw—I didn't…'

'I know it's a shock.'

He cleared his throat, gestured in the vague direction of her gently swelling stomach. 'Well, I didn't want to say…'

A smile quivered on her lips. 'No one ever does.'

'And the—the father?'

She swallowed, lifted her chin. 'It's Brendan.'

It wasn't that late, but Brendan was tired. Tired of fighting the desire to see her. Tired of fighting his love for her. Tired. Just tired.

Looking out over the London skyline, he found

himself wondering where she was, what she was doing… She'd flown back from Mustique that morning and a private car had taken both her and her sister home.

She'd tried to fight his generosity, but he'd already put the transport in place for Jessie, she could hardly refuse her own and insist her sister accept hers. So, he knew from his driver that she'd returned home safely that evening.

He wondered how she was feeling, whether the sickness had faded, whether the space he'd given her had helped or hindered where they went from here.

He and Joel made a right pair. At least Joel was making amends though, flying to New York to attend his sister's engagement party. Doing the right thing by his family, even if he wasn't quite ready to move on with his life fully. To take all that Jessie was offering and find true happiness again.

Brendan had no idea how to move forward though. At some point he needed to speak to Hannah, and the sooner the better. She hadn't fainted since that night but it didn't mean he wasn't worried about her. Her and their child.

Raking a hand through his hair, he turned away from the glass and poured himself a whisky. He'd leave her for tonight but come morning, he'd—

The sound of the private lift being called made him start. The only people with access other than him were his PA, Joyce, Charles and Hannah.

And only one of those would visit so late on a Saturday without being invited or contacting him first.

He headed towards it, his heart running away with itself as the lift slid into position and the doors opened and there she was…her skin aglow from the sun, cheeks no longer hollow, eyes bright. Stunning was too meek a word to describe her and his heart soared even as his brain descended with its caution.

'Hannah?'

'Is it true?' she blustered, striding forward and making him back up a step.

'Is what true?'

She paused in front of him, her eyes wide as she searched his face. 'That you're in love with me—' she swallowed, her voice whisper-soft as she added '—that you've always been in love with me?'

Oh, God.

His skin prickled from head to toe, blood draining from his face. He turned away, picked up his glass from the table and kept on going until he was before the window, eyes on the horizon and not her. Unable to look at her while he lied.

But still his mouth wouldn't work, the words wouldn't come…

'Brendan…' She came up behind him. 'Please tell me the truth. No more lies.'

'I've never lied to you, Hannah. Not ever.'

'Then tell me, is it true?'

'Who have you been speaking to?' Because there was only one person that knew for sure and he could see no reason why she would have spoken to him. Just the thought of him being in the same room as her put a fire back in his blood. And not the good kind.

'Why does that matter?'

He turned to look at her, took in her beauty, her vulnerability and, as his eyes dipped, taking in the gentle swell of her stomach in the dress that she wore. Her baby, his baby, theirs...

'There's only one person that ever knew my feelings for you...' His voice was unrecognisable, the desire to tell her and be done with it, the desire to tell her and have her respond in kind too much to bear.

'Leon.'

His throat bobbed as she confirmed his fears. 'When did you see him?'

'He was at my apartment when I got back. He wanted some vase but more than that he came to check that I was okay and to tell me that he's getting married.'

'I'm sorry.'

She frowned. 'Why are you sorry?'

He looked back to the glass, his eyes unseeing on the view. 'I know how much you care about appearances. That's got to sting, not even divorced yet and he's proposing marriage.'

'Don't throw those words back at me.'

'Why not? It's what you said people would say.'

'When you proposed to me.'

'But when Leon proposes so soon after your breakup, it's okay. Why? Because he's in *love*?' He couldn't keep the disdain from his voice because he was in pain. He'd offered her the same, offered to paint the perfect picture for appearances' sake and still she'd rejected him.

'No. It's okay because I don't care about Leon. Not any more and never like that.'

He snorted into his glass.

'And I believe him now when he says he's found love, that they're truly happy. He told me he didn't even know what he was missing until he found her.'

'Did he now?'

'Don't sound so bitter.'

'Bitter? I'm many things but bitter isn't one of them.'

'You don't believe him.'

'I believe him, I just can't believe that you do.'

'What if I told you I understand because I've found the same?'

His heart stuttered in his chest and, slowly, he turned to look at her, his eyes narrowed, his heart hanging on a thread. 'What are you talking about?'

She took a tentative step towards him. 'What

if I told you that I didn't know what I was missing either?'

Another step.

'What if I told you that until that night three months ago, I'd been blind to what my heart desired? You know my upbringing, you know my thoughts on love, you know why I married Leon, why I felt safe with Leon.'

'I do.' His voice was raw, as though he hadn't used it in a very long time.

'I was scared,' she confessed, pressing her hand to her heart. 'But I'm not scared any more.'

His own heart started to beat, a deep, steady thud.

'So, I'll ask you again, is it true? Did you love me?'

'Yes.'

Another step and she was almost touching him, her familiar scent teasing at his senses, his breaths too shallow but taking her in all the same.

'Do you *still* love me?'

He wet his lips. 'Hannah, don't tease me with this. If this is some test, some weird way of accepting my proposal but not—'

She touched her hand to his chest. 'No, Brendan. This is no test. No tease. Just the truth. I rejected your proposal because you did it out of convenience, because it made sense practically. I rejected you because you deserve a real marriage, you deserve love and all the happiness that comes with it. I rejected you because I realised I cared for you too much to allow you to settle for me.'

'Settle?' he choked out. 'I would never be settling, not with you.'

She lifted her hand to his cheek, her eyes hooked in his. 'Do you love me, Brendan?'

He felt as if his heart were in his throat, choking up his words, his eyes lost in the intensity of hers. 'I never stopped loving you, Hannah.'

She gave the slightest headshake, tears welling in the corners of her eyes. 'Then why didn't you tell me the truth?'

'Because I know you and I feared you'd run.' The truth came easy now. 'I gave you the proposal I thought you needed to hear, not the proposal I wanted to give.'

'Oh, Brendan, if only you'd said, if only you'd told me the truth all those weeks ago.'

'You wouldn't have been ready to hear it.'

She bit her lip. 'No, but I would have known. I would have come here sooner to tell you what I'm telling you now.'

'Are you saying you'll marry me?'

'No…'

His heart contracted, cold, unloved, but she cupped his face in her hands, the love blazing in her eyes at odds with her words.

'I'm not about to rush out tomorrow and marry you. I'm not Leon. I'm not rash or hasty or led by my heart, you know that.'

'Then what are you saying?'

'I'm saying that I love you, that against all my stupid judgement, my lifelong promise to myself, I love you and, if you'll have me, I'll happily spend the rest of my life convincing you of it.'

He'd waited fifteen years to hear her say it. He'd dreamed of it, fantasised about it, but nothing could have prepared him for the rush of love and joy he felt at hearing it.

'I'm not ready to skip down the aisle again tomorrow, Brendan, but I am ready to open my heart to you and promise you that I will love you, you and our baby, with my absolute all. If you will have me?'

'Hannah...' His voice cracked. 'That's one hell of a proposal.'

He went to kiss her and she pressed her finger to his lips. 'Do you accept?'

'Do you really need me to answer that?'

'I really do, because I've been a chicken and a fool and I wouldn't blame you if you wanted to run while you still can.'

He chuckled low in his throat. 'I think we're both done running from the truth, don't you?'

She nodded. 'So...?'

'Yes—' he hooked his arms around her, pulled her body to his '—I will have you, you and our child and any more we can possibly make. I have loved you for fifteen years and I will love you for the rest of my days, Hannah Rose. Whether you remain a Rose or a Hart, I am yours and you are mine. I love you.'

'I love you too.'

She went to kiss him but it was his turn to stop her.

'Though tell me one thing...'

'Anything?'

'Why did Leon tell you about me?'

She cocked her head to one side, her smile turning sheepish. 'I may have told him about the baby...'

'Seriously?'

'I hardly had a choice. He could already see for himself and I didn't want him having it confirmed by someone else. I owed him that.'

'How did he take it?'

'He smiled.'

'He did *what*?'

'It seems Leon now believes in fate, and, to his mind, no couple is more fated than us.'

'*Fate?* You have to be kidding me. Is this all thanks to his girlfriend, fiancée even?'

'More thanks to love.'

He gave a husky laugh. 'I'm not going to argue with that.'

'Me neither.'

And then he kissed her. Fate, chance, coincidence, whatever—he didn't care what had brought them to this point, only that it had.

* * * * *

If you missed the previous story in the
Billionaires for the Rose Sisters duet
check out

Billionaire's Island Temptation

And if you enjoyed this story,
check out these other great reads from
Rachael Stewart

My Year with the Billionaire
The Billionaire Behind the Headlines
Secrets Behind the Billionaire's Return

All available now!